Nick knew her: Katie!

The prickly brat of his memory had turned into a goddess. "You can't possibly be Katie. She was just a kid."

"I was a late developer," she informed him glacially. "I am now twenty-one years old and all of five foot three. I thought you would have recognized my face."

"And when I didn't, you kept quiet on purpose."

"You bet I did. I was hearing such interesting things about myself. Fancy calling an innocent child like me the Poison Pixie!" she seethed.

"You weren't a child. You were sixteen!"

"But you didn't know that."

"I'll tell you one thing that hasn't changed, Katie. You were a pain in the neck then, and you're a pain in the neck now."

"Ditto!"

Dear Reader,

Get ready to meet another of the world's most eligible
bachelors: they're sexy, successful and, best of all, they're
all yours!

This month in Harlequin Romance®, we bring you the latest
in the **BACHELOR TERRITORY** series. All these books
have two things in common—they're all predominantly
written from the hero's point of view and they're absolutely
wonderful!

This month's book is *Be My Girl!* by Lucy Gordon.

Happy Reading!

The Editors

**There are two sides to every story...
and now it's his turn!**

Be My Girl!
Lucy Gordon

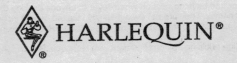

TORONTO • NEW YORK • LONDON
AMSTERDAM • PARIS • SYDNEY • HAMBURG
STOCKHOLM • ATHENS • TOKYO • MILAN • MADRID
PRAGUE • WARSAW • BUDAPEST • AUCKLAND

ISBN 0-373-03529-2

BE MY GIRL!

First North American Publication 1998.

Printed in U.S.A.

CHAPTER ONE

KATIE. Katie Deakins.

Nick tried both versions, hoping the words would bring some image to his mind, but nothing happened. The Katie he'd known had looked like any other kid. At least he thought so. He couldn't remember her appearance well enough to be sure even of that. Her hair had been—well, anyway, she'd been—or had she? All that lingered in his mind was their mutual hostility.

'What's struck you all of a heap?'

Derek, who shared Nick's expensive bachelor pad, appeared for breakfast, still showing the effects of the night before. He was in his late twenties, with merry eyes, the face of a wicked cherub, and more charm than was good for him. His eyebrows rose quizzically at the sight of the pale blue letter paper Nick was holding, and the discarded, matching envelope with its elegant writing.

'Aha! A letter from The Lady!' he observed, grinning. 'The Cruel One, whose beauty—'

'It's from my sister-in-law, if that's what you mean,' Nick said repressively.

'Same thing. Isobel, the one who sent you into a spin when you were twenty-four, nearly accepted you, then decided she preferred your brother—smart woman.'

'Cut it out,' Nick grunted.

Derek became solemn. 'I understand. After five years the heart still has its scars.'

'What were you drinking last night?'

'Can't remember,' Derek said truthfully. 'But it was a good party, though.'

'I know. I could hear it through the ceiling.'

The apartment immediately above was occupied by a group of extremely lively young women, mostly air hostesses, with a model thrown in. On the rare occasions when they were all at home they enjoyed themselves wholeheartedly.

'You should have come up and joined us,' Derek said, smiling at certain memories.

'I had work to do.'

'You always have work to do when there's any fun to be had. Why don't you lighten up? The sky won't fall just because you don't produce some banking report.'

'I'm not working on reports right now. Two of my major clients are merging and I'm trying to guide them through it with the fewest possible nervous breakdowns. But every breakdown they don't have is one that I probably *will* have. I'll lighten up when the worst is over.'

'The hell you will! You'll just start getting ready for the next crisis. Don't blame me if you have a heart attack before you're fifty. Why do you keep frowning at that letter? What's the problem?'

'You are. How can I bring an innocent young girl within a mile of you?'

'You've lost me.'

'Isobel's kid sister, Katie, is coming to London, and I'm supposed to look after her.' He scowled as Derek gave a hoot of laughter. 'It's not so damned funny——'

'It is,' Derek choked. 'Mind you,' he added, calming down, 'you're a good choice. Old before your time.'

'If you mean that I have some serious interests, and don't fill my life with women plucked from the back row of the chorus—— '

'The *front* row, do you mind? I have my standards! Nick, you're too young for serious interests. Twenty-nine, going on fifty. You even wear a tie, for Pete's sake!'

'I'm a merchant banker. I'm expected to wear a tie. We can't all swan around in jeans.'

Derek grinned, emphasising the look of a cheeky little boy. Nick, by contrast, had lean features, with dark, intense eyes, hinting at a nature that took everything a tad too seriously, including himself.

'Isobel wants me to take her "under my wing",' he groaned.

'How old is Katie?'

'Seventeenish.'

'Aha!'

'If I didn't already have misgivings, you saying "Aha!" in that voice would start them. Katie is off limits to you. I am *in loco parentis*.'

'I didn't do languages. What does that mean?'

'It means keep your lecherous hands off her.'

'Will you lighten up, for pity's sake?' Derek groaned.

That was his constant refrain to Nick. Lighten up! Don't take it all so seriously! But it fell on deaf ears.

Nick had grown up in the shadow of his older brother, Brian, a handsome giant with a ready smile and an aversion to anything between the covers of a book. He'd been sports mad, tipped to become a football star. Nick had been known as 'the bright one', and he'd worked night and day to pass exams, because it was the only thing he could do better than Brian.

He'd won scholarships, but Brian had won the girls. He'd been top of the class, but Brian had drawn smiles wherever he went. As he'd grown older, most people would have called Nick handsome. He was tall, with a hard, lean body that moved with unconscious grace. His dark, brooding looks seemed to hint at a complex inner life. His features were fine, and the slightly austere quality of his face was offset by a wide, mobile mouth whose smiles were usually unexpected, and all the more delightful for that.

He'd attracted his fair share of girlfriends, but his relationships seldom lasted. He was too serious for his age, and they left him for more entertaining partners. That had never happened to his beefily splendid brother, who drew women like bees around a honeypot and kept them entranced. Nick didn't dislike Brian, because nobody could do that. But it irked him.

The footballing career had come to nothing, and Brian had settled for owning a small sports shop in his home town. Nick had gone on to London, and success in the banking world. The habits of his childhood had stuck. There was always one more exam to pass, one more goal to achieve, before he could think about having fun.

He'd done well in his job, and had celebrated his last promotion by buying this elegant apartment high above the River Thames. His housewarming party had boasted several significant names in banking. There had also been some people he'd never seen before, one of whom had been happily asleep behind the sofa when the rest had gone. That was how he'd met Derek.

Derek was brilliant at inventing computer software, and already on his way to making a modest fortune. But he had the soul of a hobo, preferring to camp out in his friends' homes rather than put down roots in a place of his own. By that time Nick knew he'd overstretched himself on the mortgage, and he'd been glad of Derek's rent.

That had been a year ago, and they were still under

the same roof. They drove each other mad, yet neither felt any real urgency about ending the arrangement. They were chalk and cheese: the one all gravity, the other full of lightness and charm. Each was aghast at the other's lifestyle. But against the odds they'd forged a rough and ready sort of friendship that seemed to work.

Nick was ten minutes late leaving that morning, which meant he got caught in a traffic jam. It gave him time to brood on the calamity that was about to befall him.

Katie Deakins! The girl who'd practically ruined his life!

It was coming back now: Delford, the sleepy town where he'd grown up. He was fond of the cosy little place, surrounded by beautiful countryside and close to his parents, whom he visited often.

On a trip home he'd met Isobel, and been instantly entranced by her fair, pastel beauty. She'd been two years older, but what did age matter? With every day he'd fallen more deeply in love. Isobel was a doctor, newly employed by the local practice. Her parents had divorced and her father lived in Australia. Since their mother's death Isobel had raised her kid sister, Katie.

And whoever had named that child knew what they were doing, Nick thought. Talk about a little shrew!

Now he remembered what she looked like: small and angular, with long hair falling all over her elfin face.

Why had she disliked him so much? At first he'd thought she was being possessive about Isobel. He had furious memories of bribing her to clear off so that he could be alone with his beloved, then seeing her reappear early, daring him to object.

He'd booked a weekend away, a special time for Isobel and himself, to lift their relationship onto a more beautiful plane. And it had come to nothing because the

wretched child had developed a stomach ache that kept
Isobel at home. Nick had been deeply cynical about that
illness. It hadn't stopped her climbing trees.

Everyone else had found her delightful, he remembered. So might he, if they hadn't been at daggers drawn
over Isobel. Katie had had a passionate protectiveness
that led her to take in waifs and strays. She'd filled her
home with elderly animals that she'd cared for lovingly.
She would pick up babies and snuggle her face against
them with little gurgles of delight.

But it had been different with Nick. Katie seemed to
have taken one look at him and decided *Yuk!* Thereafter
her hobby had been winding him up and letting him
down.

Memories came fast now: introducing Isobel to Brian,
the way they'd smiled at each other. The sinking feeling
in his stomach.

And then the afternoon when he'd called at her house,
to find her in the kitchen in her dressing gown, while
Brian stood behind her, bare chested, nuzzling her neck
in a contented manner that told its own story. When
they'd seen him Isobel had blushed and said, 'I'm sorry,
Nick...'

Brian hadn't said anything, just stood there with a
sheepish grin on his face.

And Katie? Where had she been when she might have
done something useful? Nowhere. Just vanished, and
leaving them a clear field, as she'd never done for himself.

To add insult to injury, Katie had liked Brian. He
hadn't even had to bribe her to make herself scarce that
fateful afternoon. So she hadn't been trying to obstruct
all her sister's suitors. Just Nick.

Of course he'd got over it, after a fashion. It was only

in melodrama that a man nursed a grudge for years. In real life he'd made the best of things, danced at their wedding and become godfather to their children. And as time had passed he'd faced the fact that he hadn't really been betrayed. Brian and Isobel had fallen in love at first sight, and it was nobody's fault. But she lived in his heart as a feminine ideal, against which all other women would be measured and found wanting.

At the wedding Katie had looked wildly uncomfortable in the blue satin of a bridesmaid. He'd been equally awkward as best man, done up in formal togs, nobly nursing a broken heart. Isobel had been all sweet sympathy, even giving him a special kiss, full of understanding for his suffering. Brian had regarded them cheerfully, not even having the decency to be jealous. Katie had watched too, and he could have sworn the little wretch had smirked.

It was a long time since he'd seen Katie. She'd gone to visit her father in Australia, and stayed for three years. Nick returned to Delford each Christmas, and spent the season being clambered over by his nephews and nieces. There were three of them now, and another on the way. They were contented times, with the past apparently buried.

But to the end of his days he would wonder if things might have been different, but for Katie.

The thought of having to look after her was appalling. He would call Isobel and explain that she must make other plans. The traffic had ground to a halt again, and he seized the chance to use the car phone. Even now he felt a jolt of pleasure at the sound of her voice; soft, husky, charmingly feminine.

'Dear Nick, you got my letter. It's such a comfort to me to know that I can turn to you for help.'

'You know I'm always here for you. It's just that—'

'You're such a pet. Oh, Nick, can I confide in you?'

'Of course you can,' he said, once more helpless in her toils.

'Katie worries me since she returned from Australia. She thinks she's grown up, but she's really so young. She's set her heart on visiting London—'

'You ought to stop her coming here, Isobel.'

'My dear, I know it, but I can't. If I oppose her she'll run away and sleep rough, or get in with bad company. It won't be easy for you, looking after her. She's growing a little wild, and you'll have to watch her like a hawk.'

'What about when I'm at work? Are you sure this is such a good—?'

'Actually, it'll be a relief to get her away from one young man. She keeps telling him she's not interested, but he won't take the hint. His name's Jake Ratchett, so look out for him, won't you?'

'Isobel, I—'

'Dearest Nick, thank you for coming to my rescue. It's such a weight off my mind.'

'You know I'll do anything for you,' he said, casting resolution to the wind.

'A week or two should get it out of her system. You will keep her right under your eye, won't you?'

'Of course.'

'Make sure she doesn't stay out too late?'

'Trust me.'

'Could you bear to take her out a few times yourself, just to be on the safe side?'

'For you, I'll even do that.'

'Her train arrives at five-thirty tomorrow evening. I'll tell her you'll meet it.'

'Isobel—'

'I must dash now. The baby's crying. Brian sends his love. Bye, pet.'

Patsy Cornell ran Nick's life. Officially she was his secretary, and in front of clients she called him 'Mr Kenton', or even 'sir'. But this was a smokescreen. She was a widow in her fifties, with two grown sons and four grandsons, and a hearty disrespect for all men. A series of good investments had left her comfortably off, and she could have afforded to retire. But her sons had both flown the nest, and she enjoyed working.

After thirty years with Devenham & Wentworth, what she didn't know about merchant banking wasn't worth knowing. Nick freely acknowledged his debt to her, which was greatly to the credit of his heart, but even more to the credit of Patsy's tact.

Although she was plump and cheerful, her eyes were full of sharp intelligence, and her shrewdness could be disconcerting. When Nick invited her to lunch at the best restaurant in London she knew exactly how to value this tribute.

'What are you going to try to talk me into?' she asked her boss as soon as they were seated, and her favourite aperitif was on the table. Despite her suspicious tone, there was a twinkle in her eye.

Nick decided to take the bull by the horns. 'I want you to move into my flat.'

'Why, Nick, how flattering! But I'm not looking for a toy boy. Besides, you aren't my type. Now, if it had been that gorgeous friend of yours—'

'Why do women talk about Derek like that?' Nick demanded irritably.

'It's his cheeky little boy charm. Irresistible.'

'That's just the problem. I want you to put yourself between Derek's so-called charm and a young lady whose moral welfare has been entrusted to my care.'

Patsy gave a hoot of disrespectful laughter. 'Tell me everything,' she said eagerly.

Over the excellent lunch he laid his troubles before her.

'You really did take agin this poor child,' she protested.

'Patsy, you don't understand,' he pleaded. 'This wasn't a child as the term is commonly understood. This was an alien being from the Planet Tharg, landed on earth for the sole purpose of wrecking my life.'

Patsy choked slightly over her asparagus. 'Stop talking like an ignorant bachelor. What you've just described *is* a child as the term is commonly understood. My two were just like that.'

Nick shook his head. 'Nope. This one definitely wasn't humanoid. Her elbows were knives. I know, because she kept digging them into me. She used to make dreadful punning jokes, yell, ''How about that, then? *Boom! Boom!*'' and jab my ribs. I've still got the bruises.'

'But surely she won't be doing that at seventeen?'

'I wouldn't put anything past her,' he said gloomily.

Patsy struggled to keep a straight face. 'How old were you when all this happened?'

'Twenty-four. Why?'

'Just as I thought. Something weird happens to men at twenty-four. They start telling themselves, quite wrongly, that they're mature now, and entitled to some respect. Katie sent you up rotten and it got under your skin.'

A rueful grin broke over Nick's face, making it delightful. 'Hell, Patsy, it's not that! Well, maybe a bit.

But seriously, she's at an awkward age, and London is a dangerous place for a naive young girl.'

'Can't Lilian help? She's supposed to be your girl-friend.'

'My relationship with Lilian is at an early stage,' Nick said carefully. 'I don't think it could survive any hideous shocks. It'll only be for a couple of weeks, but I've promised Isobel that I'll keep Katie right under my eye, so she'll have to stay at the flat.'

'Ah! Near the gorgeous Derek.'

'Near Derek. Exactly. How could I ever look Isobel in the eyes again if Katie got into trouble? And then I thought—' His tone became coaxing.

'You thought of me,' she finished, amused.

'With your well-known heart of gold. You wouldn't leave me in the lurch, would you, Patsy?'

She considered. 'I'd have to bring Horace.'

Horace was Patsy's cat, a long-haired Persian with a foul temper. Nick had met him once, when Patsy had brought him to the office for a few days because he was ailing and needed a pill at four-hour intervals. Horace was elderly, wayward in his habits, adored his mistress and hated the rest of creation. Everyone had been glad when he was well enough to be left at home.

'Horace will be welcome,' Nick said, not truthfully, but with resignation.

'In that case I'll move in straight away.'

'Bless you for saving my life!'

'Bless you for saving mine! I'd been wondering if I could afford that cruise to the Bahamas.'

Nick stopped with his glass halfway to his mouth. 'I beg your pardon?'

'Being on duty night and day should earn me a nice fat bonus.'

'What about your heart of gold?'

'Have you checked the price of gold lately?'

Prompt on time the next evening, Nick was at the station to meet Katie's train. Determined to do his duty, he'd set aside the whole evening for her. He would treat her to a meal, behave with careful politeness, explain the rules of the house, and take her home to cocoa and cookies.

The train was on time, and he placed himself at the barrier. But his fixed smile faded as the crowd passed him with no sign of anyone who might be Katie. At last the platform was empty.

'She missed the damned train,' he muttered in outrage. 'I might have known!'

He returned to his parked car, meaning to call Isobel. A sleek red sports car was just gliding in beside him. A young man got out and opened the passenger door to usher out a goddess. That was the only word for her. She had a delicate face, with small, perfect features and mysterious green eyes. A mass of light brown hair, just touched with copper, flowed in waves over her shoulders. Her dainty figure was sheathed in an expensive linen trouser suit that clung to her subtly curved hips. Her white shirt was pure silk, and about her neck hung a silver chain. Nick held his breath.

'There's no need to wait with me, Freddy, dear.' Her voice had a soft, breathy quality that did funny things to Nick's spine.

'Of course I'll wait,' the young man said. He was well set up, and spoke heartily. 'I can't leave you to face the enemy alone.'

Her bubbling laugh stopped Nick's hand on the way

to the phone. He listened, for the sheer pleasure of hearing her voice, as she said, 'He's not exactly the enemy.'

'You always made him sound a monster.'

'I'm a big girl. I can take care of myself, even with monsters.'

'Darling, you're so sweet and brave. You must call me at once if he gets heavy with you.'

'It means so much to know I can rely on you,' she said earnestly.

She's got him just where she wants him, Nick thought, amused. Poor devil!

At last the eager suitor was persuaded to depart. The goddess turned and faced Nick. A pleasurable shiver went through him as he met her eyes, gleaming with laughter.

'What would you have done if he hadn't left?' he asked with a grin.

'I'd have persuaded him somehow.'

Of course she would, he thought. She'd been born to wrap men around her little finger.

'Have you been stood up, too?' he asked.

'I beg your pardon?'

'The man you're meeting—"the enemy". There doesn't seem to be any sign of him.' He saw an odd, quizzical look come into her eyes. It was charming. 'Can I buy you a coffee while you wait for him?'

Her look deepened into a puzzled frown. 'Can you—?'

'Unless you have to dash off to catch a train?'

'Aren't you—meeting someone?' she asked slowly.

'I'm supposed to be, but she hasn't shown. I might have known she'd let me down!'

'Who?'

'My brother's kid sister-in-law. I let myself be talked

into playing Mother Hen to the brat while she's in London, and I must have been mad. Still, she hasn't turned up, so with any luck, maybe she won't.'

'You never know,' she agreed, looking at him curiously. 'Yes, I'll have that coffee, thanks.'

'Great. But first I'd better call her sister and find out what happened.'

'Why bother?' the goddess asked quickly. 'She's probably on the next train. Call later. I want to hear all about you.'

When they were seated in the cheerful coffee bar, he said, 'I'm Nick.'

'I'm—I'm Jennifer.'

'You don't seem very sure.'

'My parents believed in giving their daughters a variety of first names. I've got five. Mary, Jennifer, Alice, and a couple of others. I pick and choose, depending on my mood.'

'And you're Jennifer today?'

There was a glint in her eyes that he didn't understand. 'I'm Jennifer right this minute. Tell me about the brat. I think you must be a most generous person to let yourself be talked into looking after her.'

'Well, it won't be for long. I suppose I can endure a couple of weeks. If you care for someone, you'll do things for them.'

Her eyes were sympathetic, and he found himself talking about Isobel. Now and then Jennifer nodded in perfect comprehension. In fact, there was something about her that reminded Nick of Isobel. Not physically, for they didn't look at all alike. But in the aura of warmth and understanding that she carried with her.

'You know what I think?' she said when she'd heard him out. 'I think you're still in love with Isobel.'

'Well—maybe a little. She's just a sort of ideal for me, someone that no other woman can match. I certainly wouldn't look after the Poison Pixie for anyone else.'

'The *what*?'

He grinned. 'It's just come back to me. I used to call Katie the Poison Pixie.'

The goddess spoke in a strangely tight voice. 'What did she do to deserve that?'

'Don't get me started.'

'I'll bet you didn't dare say it to her face!'

'Right! She'd have put live eels in my bed. No, I kept it inside the safety of my head. Anyway, she had rude names for me too, and she did use them out loud.'

A disconcerting change had come over the goddess. The gleam in her eye as she regarded him was definitely unfriendly.

'But she had a secret name for you, too,' she said. 'One you never knew of. *Nasty Nick!*'

'What?'

'Nasty Nick,' she said, breathing hard. 'Noxious Nick! You never suspected!'

'What—are you talking about?'

'Think about it! I know everything about you, Nick. I know that you only eat grapefruit for breakfast, and you read late at night because you don't need much sleep. I even know that you've got one foot half a size larger than the other.'

'How can you possibly know all that?' he asked in a hollow voice.

But he didn't need to ask. The scales fell from his eyes, and with a terrible sinking feeling he knew her: his nemesis, his evil genius, his black shadow.

Katie!

CHAPTER TWO

IT WAS Katie. The prickly brat of his memory had turned into the goddess. And he'd told her—what *hadn't* he told her? Nick groaned as he recalled some of the highlights of their conversation.

'Wait a minute,' he said, fighting a desperate rear-guard action. 'You can't possibly be Katie. She was—'

'Yes?' she asked ominously. 'Be careful what you say!'

'Katie was— I know it's been five years, but nobody could change that much—you were just a kid.'

'I was sixteen.'

'You couldn't have been.'

'Don't tell me how old I was!'

'Well, you only looked about thirteen.'

'I was a late developer,' she informed him glacially. 'I was thin for my age, and short. I've made up for it since. I am now twenty-one years old and all of five foot three.'

'Well, is that my fault?' he demanded illogically.

'You didn't even have the decency to recognise my face.'

'How could I recognise your face? I've hardly ever seen it before. You kept it permanently covered by a mane of hair. Talking to you was like trying to communicate with an ill-tempered mop. And that was on your good days.'

'Don't make excuses.'

'I'm not making excuses,' Nick said patiently. 'I'm

merely explaining why you're completely in the wrong about this.'

'Well, that's one thing that hasn't changed. You always did act like a man bringing the word down from the mountain. I don't know how Isobel put up with you.'

'Kindly don't change the subject.'

'I don't know what the subject is, except that you're on your high horse, as usual.'

'I don't like being set up—'

'I did no such thing.'

'Oh, no? I suppose it wasn't setting me up to arrive by car when I was meeting a train?'

'That was an accident. I meant to get here before the train. I would have done if Freddy hadn't got lost. I thought you'd recognise me at once.'

'And when I didn't, you kept quiet on purpose.'

'You bet I did! I was hearing such interesting things about myself.'

'And I suppose giving me a false name wasn't setting me up—*Jennifer*?'

'I never gave you a false name. Like I said, I have several. Jennifer was the one I was using at that moment.'

'How was I supposed to know that you had several names?'

'Because I told you so once before. Mary, Jennifer and Alice are family names. We all have them, including Isobel. I explained all this one evening when you'd called for her and she was upstairs getting ready. And do you know what you said? *"Uhuh!"* That was your stock answer to every remark I made. I played fair with you today. I gave you clues.'

'What I don't understand is how you persuaded Isobel not to warn me that you were coming by car.'

'She didn't know. I wanted to surprise you—'

'Catch me out, you mean.'

'It never occurred to me that you wouldn't know me, but I'm glad now that it happened. I wouldn't have missed today for anything in the world. How dare you tell people I was the Poison Pixie?'

'And how dare you tell Freddy I was the enemy?'

'I think I got that about right!'

As they glared at each other the years rolled back. They were at daggers drawn again, as though it were yesterday.

'Fancy calling an innocent child the Poison Pixie!' she seethed.

'If you were innocent, Attila the Hun was a misunderstood delinquent! And you weren't a child. You were sixteen!'

'But you didn't know that.'

'That's irrelevant!' he snapped.

'Oh, no, it isn't!'

'I'll tell you one thing that hasn't changed, Katie. You were a pain in the neck then, and you're a pain in the neck now.'

'Ditto!'

Hostilities were put into abeyance while they had dinner. Nick had booked an early table at an Italian restaurant, which met with Katie's hearty approval. Her arrival caused a small sensation, and two young waiters almost came to blows for the privilege of serving her.

'Why are you so gloomy?' she asked over the spaghetti.

'I'm not gloomy. I'm just thinking hard. When I made plans I was imagining you as little more than a child. Obviously that has to change.'

She gave a delighted little chuckle. 'You made plans for me? How nice! What were they?'

'Oh, the usual things, like seeing the sights.'

'Are you going to take me to see the Tower of London?' she teased.

'You should certainly see it, but you won't need an escort. I'll buy you a map and a good guidebook, and you're on your own.'

'You mean you aren't coming with me?'

'Not a chance.'

'You're going to turn me out alone in the big, bad city?' Katie asked, shocked. 'Suppose I was set upon, spirited away and never seen again—'

'I should be so lucky!'

'Kidnapped and held to ransom—'

'I'd pay them to keep you,' he said firmly.

Her theatrical pose collapsed and her cheeky grin acknowledged a point to him. Then she set about winding a long strand of spaghetti on her fork, without letting any go astray. Watching this talented performance, Nick had to admit that she was one of the few women he knew who could eat spaghetti gracefully.

'What did *you* have in mind when you thought of this trip?' he asked.

'Oh, this and that,' she said vaguely. 'A bit of sightseeing, theatres, buying clothes, and lots and lots of fun.'

'It's going to be a crowded two weeks.'

'I'll probably need more than two weeks.'

His spine tingled with alarm. 'Isobel definitely told me two weeks at the most.'

'We-ell, I may have given her that impression. But I'll actually need longer.'

'How much longer?' he asked in a hollow voice.

'Don't know. It depends how much fun I'm having. I

think I've earned it. I've spent the last few years working so hard.' Her sigh suggested Cinderella.

'Doing what?'

'Helping out on Dad's sheep farm. It's a little place, without enough people to run it, so I had to slave. Up at dawn, work till dusk, then drop. That's been my life. You don't know what it means to me to be in a big city at last. Kind of overwhelming, really.'

He was about to sympathise. Just in time he caught the teasing glint in Katie's eyes.

'Cut it out,' he commanded. 'You've been living in Sydney and your father's allergic to wool.'

'Fancy you knowing that,' she said admiringly.

'Isobel mentioned it.

'Ah, well, of course, if Isobel told you!' she said significantly.

He felt himself colouring. 'I think we'd better just forget anything that was said at the station.'

'Don't worry, you didn't actually admit you were still in love with her. I guessed it for myself.'

'Then you guessed wrong,' he said, in a low, furious voice.

'You didn't see your own face. You're still nutty about her.'

'Stop talking nonsense. Isobel is my brother's wife!'

'But she belonged to you first. At least, she didn't actually—'

'No, you saw to that,' he muttered.

'Pardon?'

'Nothing. Once and for all, I am not in love with Isobel.'

'You're not?'

'Certainly not.'

'Then what are you doing here with me?' she demanded, with the air of a magician producing a rabbit from a hat. 'It's not from choice, is it? If you weren't trying to impress my sister with your faithful devotion I could sleep in a garbage bin for all you cared.'

This was so close to the truth that he could only glare at her.

'Come on, admit it!' she challenged. 'You don't want me here—'

'No prizes for guessing that. Why should I want you here, interrupting my work, taking up my time? But you're Brian's sister-in-law, and you're still very young. Isobel asked me to keep you out of trouble, and that's what I'm going to do.'

Her eyes glinted. 'I wonder if you'll manage it, Nick.'

He would have given a lot to know the answer to that himself.

'You seem never to have heard of things like family loyalty, and duty,' he grumbled, trying to regain the initiative.

'Aha! I'm a *duty*!'

'Well, you sure as hell aren't a pleasure!' he snapped.

She gave a little gasp. 'What a terrible thing to say to me. I've come all the way from the other side of the world—it was such a long, tiring journey. But I kept thinking of my family waiting for me—and instead I've just walked into a brick wall of rejection—' She sniffed and her eyes were suspiciously bright.

'Come on, Katie, I didn't mean to upset you.'

'I know.' She dabbed her eyes. 'I guess it's not your fault you're insensitive, Nick. Nature just made you that way. You can't imagine what it's like being so far away—dreaming of people—'

'Well, you weren't dreaming of me, were you? Not unless you were sticking pins into my image.' He saw the tears rolling unchecked down her cheeks, and was appalled. 'Katie!' he pleaded. 'Don't cry. I didn't mean it like that. I'm sorry if I was unkind.'

'Honestly, Nick, it's like taking candy from a baby,' she said, with a complete change of tone. She surveyed him from eyes that were dry and full of amusement. 'You shouldn't let me fool you that easily.'

'Why, you little—' He breathed hard, but after a moment a reluctant grin came over his face. 'I should have remembered you can cry to order.'

'Yes, among all my other sins, I think you should have remembered that one,' she agreed amiably.

'You wretched girl! What am I going to do with you'?

'Feed me, feed me! Where's that *pesca ripiena* I was promised?'

There was a rush to serve her. One waiter whisked away her plate, and another produced stuffed peaches and refilled her wine glass. She rewarded them both with a dazzling smile, and they bowed their way out worshipfully.

'Plenty of young men in Australia, were there?' Nick asked, appreciating this little display of power.

'Possibly. I didn't notice,' she said airily.

'Or did you lose count?'

'No, I don't think I had *that* many.'

'If what I'm watching in here tonight is any guide, I should think you probably did have that many,' he said wryly.

'Whatever do you—? Oh, the waiters,' she said with an air of innocence that didn't fool him. 'You don't mean that *I'm* the one who's got them fumbling around like that?'

'Don't play the innocent with me. They don't see a face like yours every day.'

She gave him a sunny smile. 'Am I really pretty, Nick?'

'You're passable,' he said, refusing to rise to the bait.

'Shame on you!'

'Don't play your tricks on me. Save that for impressionable boys. As long as you're here, I'm standing in for your father.'

'Surely you're not *that* much older than me?'

'No, I'm not "that much older than you",' he said edgily. 'But Isobel raised you, and I nearly married her.'

'Oh, no, you didn't. You never stood a chance.'

He ground his teeth. 'We won't discuss this, if you please.'

'You started it, talking about standing in for my father. You shouldn't put yourself down, Nick. You're not all that bad. Not really.'

'Just finish your peaches, will you?' he said, speaking with difficulty.

'I'm only kidding. You don't begrudge me my little joke, do you?'

'Yes.'

She poured cream over her peaches with a generous hand.

'I thought young women didn't eat like that any more,' he said. 'Isn't it all low fat foods and watching your weight?'

'Oh, I never bother about my weight,' she said airily. 'I just eat what I like and I seem to stay the same.' She became suddenly alarmed. 'You don't think I'm getting fat, do you?' She looked down at herself, pressing the silk shirt back against her body and smoothing her hands over her snugly clad hips.

'You're all right,' he said, unable to avoid studying her perfect figure.

'Are you sure? I mean, look at me properly.'

'I *am* looking at you properly.'

It was strange how physically unlike Isobel she was. Both sisters were fair, but Isobel's fairness was like milk, while Katie's had the richness of cream. Isobel was a poem in soft pastel shades. Katie glowed with vivid life. Even her lack of height couldn't dim the radiance she carried with her.

Satisfied about her figure, Katie returned to eating. 'Isobel says you're a big man in banking now,' she said.

'I work for an old established merchant banker, and I do pretty well.'

'Why must you be so prosaic about it? What about the romance of banking?'

'The *what*?'

'Driving the engine of commerce,' she said theatrically. 'Making the wheels go round. Isobel made you sound like a real big shot.'

'Really?' He tried not to sound as pleased as he felt.

'Luxury flat with a view of the river. I'm longing to see it.'

'We'll go home as soon as you're finished. Patsy's looking forward to meeting you.'

Her reaction was strange. Her face paled, and she asked faintly, 'Patsy?'

'She's my secretary. You'll like her. She mothers me, and she'll mother you.'

'That sounds nice.' Katie had recovered her poise.

'She's staying with us while you're here.'

'Whatever for? In case I have designs on your person? Tell her not to worry.'

'Stop trying to wind me up. And it's time I told you about Derek. He's my lodger—'

'Young?'

'Yes.'

'Good-looking?'

'Women seem to think so. If you're wise you'll give him a miss.'

'That'll be hard if we're sharing a roof.'

'That's why Patsy's there.'

Katie dissolved into laughter. 'Nick, you're protecting my virtue. How lovely!'

'Katie, even in this day and age a young woman can't share a flat with two men without people thinking the worst.'

'Not if they're both as stuffy as you. Relax!'

'If Derek was like me I'd have no problems,' he growled.

'Nick, if there were any more like you, the *world* would have problems.'

'Can we be serious?'

'I was being serious. Tell me about Derek. Is he a banker too?'

'No, he's a computer genius. He invents software, and it's damned good. But his character might kindly be described as "wayward". He likes to think of himself as a man who eats the Apple of Life. Personally I think he's planted the pips and grown his own orchard.'

Too late he realised he'd said the wrong thing. Katie's eyes were gleaming. 'He sounds yummy! When do I get to meet him?'

Nick decided he must pull himself together. He'd been caught off guard by the change in Katie, and it was causing him to make all the wrong moves.

It was her fault, sitting there looking glorious, with that warm sheen on her skin and those wide, beautiful green eyes with their hint of mysterious depths. Derek would go wild when he saw her.

Nick felt ill-used. He'd been prepared for an awkward Katie, a rebellious Katie, a troublesome Katie. But no one had warned him about a beautiful Katie. Now the situation had all the makings of a disaster, for which Isobel would blame him.

'You'll meet him when he gets home tonight,' he said. 'Assuming that he bothers to come home and sleep in his own bed.'

'He sounds fascinating. Besides, anyone you disapprove of can't be all bad.'

'Thank you,' he snapped.

'He might be my type.'

'He isn't any sensible girl's type.'

'But when was I ever sensible? Isobel was the sensible one, and even she—' Katie stopped, looking at him sideways from under the longest lashes Nick had ever seen.

'What?' he urged.

'Never mind.'

'What were you going to say about Isobel?'

'Only that she threw her cap over the windmill when Brian came along. He brought out her ''unsensible'' side, and I think that was what she secretly wanted.'

'If you've finished eating,' he said frostily, 'we should be going.'

On the journey home he thawed towards her again. It was Katie's first trip to London, and her eager enjoyment was touching. Even so, his patience was tested when she begged him to stop the car so that she could look at a dress in a shop window, and then blithely hopped out, leaving him frantically trying to find a parking space. By the time he'd parked and walked back to the shop she'd bought the dress and was hugging it to her, eyes shining.

'Did it blow much of a hole in your budget?' he asked.

She told him.

'How much?'

'I know it was extravagant, but it was an exclusive model and the very last one they had. And I love it so. It was simply made for me.'

'Well, as long as you're happy,' he said indulgently.

He offered to carry the shiny bag to the car, but she clutched it to her and shook her head, refusing to be parted from her treasure.

She was thrilled by his apartment, especially the wall of windows that looked out over London. It was growing dark, and the lights on the river made an entrancing spectacle.

To Nick's dismay there was no sign of Patsy, but she arrived almost at once, looking a little flustered.

'I'm sorry,' she said in a low voice. 'I had to dash out to get some of Horace's special food. His stomach always plays him up in unfamiliar surroundings.'

'Where is he now?' Nick asked nervously.

'Sulking behind the sofa. Don't worry. He'll stay there for ages.'

Katie had been gazing rapturously out of the window, oblivious to this conversation, but she turned quickly when Patsy said, 'You must be Katie. I've looked forward to meeting you.'

Nick made the introductions, glad to see that the two women seemed to take to each other. Patsy could hardly hide her surprise at the vision before her, and quickly took Katie into the room they were to share.

'Nick's told me a lot about you,' she said as they did Katie's unpacking together. 'But none of it quite seems to describe you.'

'That was five years ago,' Katie said cheerfully. 'Nick's forgotten a lot. And there's also a good deal he doesn't know.' She gave Patsy a wink.

'I see,' Patsy said. 'At least, I think I see.'

'Tell me about him,' Katie begged. 'What's he like at work?'

'Very correct. Very proper. Everything has to be just the way he wants it.'

'I can imagine.'

'But if that were all he'd be dull to work for, and he isn't dull. Sometimes there's a flash of another man, with imagination and flair. The trouble is, Nick won't give that man free reign.'

'What about girlfriends?' Katie asked casually.

'He's had his fair share. Nick's never had trouble attracting women because he's so good-looking—'

'Good-looking?' Katie interrupted with a little frown. 'Do you think so?'

'Don't you?'

'I never thought him more than moderate,' Katie said casually.

A faint puzzled look appeared in Patsy's eyes, then vanished, replaced by a look of understanding.

'So he's got lots of girlfriends?' Katie continued.

'Not all at one time, and they don't last, because he doesn't seem to get deeply involved with them. Although—'

Nick knocked on the door and looked in. 'I'm making us a snack—hey, is that the famous dress?'

Katie had laid her new purchase lovingly out on her bed. It was a long, silken dress in the colours of autumn. Even Nick, who knew nothing of such matters, could see that it was made for her vivid beauty.

'Wow!' he said appreciatively.

'Do you really like it?' she asked eagerly. 'It will suit me, won't it?'

'Bound to, I should say,' he responded, amused by her fervour.

'Have I got time for a shower?'

She darted across the hall into the bathroom, and they heard the sound of running water.

'She's charming,' Patsy told Nick, leading the way out of the bedroom. 'Much nicer than you said. Alien from Tharg, indeed!'

'That's just a disguise to fool you,' he said with a grin. 'Underneath she's a huge insect with spaghetti growing out of her head.' He went back to the living area. 'No sign of Derek?'

'He's out with a young lady,' Patsy said. 'I'm not sure when he'll be back.'

'Let's hope it's a nice long time.'

For once, he felt, the heavens were smiling on him. But he should have known better. It was somehow inevitable that Derek should bounce through the front door five minutes later, calling, 'Well, have you collected the vampire brat yet? Is she as dreadful as you said?'

'Shut up!' Nick told him frantically.

But it was too late. The door of the bathroom clicked, and Katie stood there. 'Why don't you judge for yourself?' she asked in a teasing voice.

Even Nick had to admit that she looked stunning, clad only in a towel, her glorious hair tumbling over her bare shoulders. The towel wasn't quite large enough for its job, only just covering her breasts and revealing most of her slim, perfect legs. Derek gulped audibly, and Nick reckoned it served him right.

'That's not fair,' Derek said at last, sounding as though he was having trouble breathing. 'It's cheating.'

'I always cheat,' Katie replied in a husky voice. 'It's the surest way to win.' She gave him a slow, luxurious smile, and Derek dropped his car keys.

'You can have me as first prize any time,' he said.

Staring disaster in the face, Nick acted quickly. His own towelling bathrobe hung behind the door, and in a moment he'd whisked it over Katie's shoulders, turning her so that he could pull the edges together and hold them there.

She laughed up at him, her elusive perfume rising tantalisingly around his head, her delicate body pressed against his. 'You were supposed to be having a shower,' he said firmly. 'So why don't you get back in there and have it?'

'But you haven't introduced me to your friend,' she pointed out.

'Later.' He was urging her back into the bathroom. 'Later.'

'Can't I meet him now?'

'Much later.' He got the bathroom door closed.

'Spoilsport,' Derek jeered.

To Nick's relief, when Katie next appeared she was fully dressed in black trousers and a peacock-blue sleeveless sweater. Nick made proper introductions, and Derek took Katie's hand with reverence.

'You don't know how pleased I am to meet you,' he said slowly.

'Me too. I've been dying to meet you ever since Nick told me about you today.'

Derek gave a wide grin. 'Whatever he said, I'll bet it wasn't flattering.'

'I'm afraid it wasn't,' Katie admitted sadly. 'In fact, I can't imagine even half of it was true.'

'What did you tell her, you dog?' Derek demanded.

'Never mind,' Katie protested sweetly. 'It'll be much more fun finding out the truth for myself.'

'That's a great idea.'

Nick watched this exchange with tolerant cynicism. 'Just you be careful,' he warned Derek. 'One minute you'll think you're doing fine, and the next you'll find you've fallen into one of her traps.'

'Would you like a snack?' Patsy asked, offering Katie a plate of toast.

'I daren't,' she said sadly. 'I've already eaten, and, anyway. Nick says I'm too fat.'

'I never—'

'You did, Nick. You know you did. In the restaurant you practically accused me of stuffing myself. Well, maybe I was eating a little bit much, but it was my first meal of the day, and I was starving.' She appealed pathetically to the other two. 'I didn't think he'd mind feeding me a little extra, but he did.'

'*Katie!*' Nick said wrathfully.

'He always was a mean old skinflint,' Derek agreed.

'You don't think I'm fat, do you?' she asked, turning so that he could appreciate her from all angles.

'Just perfect,' he said fervently.

Patsy said nothing. It was taking all her efforts to keep a straight face.

Driven beyond endurance, Nick seized Katie's arm and drew her against him, looking down into her charming face.

'You haven't changed a bit, have you?' he demanded in a low, furious voice. 'You're still the same devious, double dealing little horror you always were.'

'You're more right than you know, Nick,' she said softly. 'I haven't changed a bit—not one little bit.'

'And just what does that mean?'

'You'll find out.' Then she smiled right up into his face, and he had the strangest sensation that the sun had come out.

He released her, finding that it was impossible to stay mad at Katie, even for him. He hadn't realised before how dull his apartment could be. Perhaps a bright, vibrant young woman couldn't be blamed for wanting to cheer the place up with a bit of teasing. After that he fell in with her mood, and the party became very merry.

CHAPTER THREE

AT LAST Nick yawned, thinking of the mountain of work that awaited him tomorrow.

'Yes, it's late, isn't it?' Patsy said, looking at her watch in surprise. 'I'll just collect Horace and— He's gone.' She was looking behind an armchair that stood in the corner.

'He can't have got out of the flat,' Nick said easily. 'He'll turn up.'

He froze as an ominous sound reached them all. It came from inside Katie and Patsy's room, and it unmistakably indicated a cat whose stomach had rebelled.

'Oh, no!' Patsy cried, going pale and rushing to the bedroom door, which had been left ajar. Katie raced to catch up with her, and gave a little scream at the sight that met her eyes. Nick, following them into the room, groaned and covered his eyes.

Horace sat defiantly in the middle of Katie's dress, his rejected supper staining the silk. The beautiful garment, bought so lovingly only a few hours before, was ruined.

'Oh, Horace!' Patsy wailed. 'Katie, I'm sorry! He's mine. How could I have been so careless?'

'I was the careless one,' Nick said grimly. 'I left this room last, and I should have shut the door.' He ground his teeth. 'I should have realised that *that dratted animal*—'

'Don't shout at him!' Katie cried indignantly. 'You'll frighten him.'

'*What?*' He wasn't sure he'd heard properly.

Katie ignored him, scooped up Horace, holding him gently, and said, 'Poor baby! You're not well, are you? What have you been eating?'

'He's quite old,' Patsy said cautiously, as though hardly able to believe her ears. 'Strange surroundings upset him. I should have watched him more carefully.'

'Perhaps if we warmed some milk, that would settle his stomach?' Katie suggested, tickling the miscreant under the chin.

'But—your dress—' Patsy said, almost believing that Katie hadn't noticed the damage. 'He's torn it as well as making a mess of it.'

Katie gave a rueful look at the garment. 'Well, it can't be helped,' she said with a sigh. 'I ought to have hung it up.'

'I'll replace it,' Patsy said. 'He's my cat.'

'*I'll* replace it,' Nick said firmly. 'I left the door open.'

'Let's worry about that later,' Katie said, stroking Horace, who snuggled against her, purring like a foghorn. 'Warm milk for you, my darling, and then you'll feel better.'

Patsy gave Nick a speaking glance, and murmured, when Katie was out of earshot, 'Don't you ever dare slander that sweet, generous girl to me again.'

'I remember now,' he said wryly. 'She was always nuts about animals.'

'She'd really have to be nuts to brush aside the ruin of a beautiful creation like that. Nick, is it really irreplaceable?'

'I think so.'

'You ought to be ashamed of yourself,' Patsy said. 'I wouldn't have reacted so well.'

Nick was feeling all at sea. In the first instant he'd caught the look on Katie's face. She was no saint, and she'd reacted to the destruction of her new dress like any normal red-blooded girl. She'd wanted to do murder.

But that had vanished in a flash, swallowed up by her pity for the old cat and an instinctive tenderness for Patsy's feelings. It reminded him of what he'd known years before, that alongside teasing, tormenting Katie was kindly, warm-hearted Katie. To everyone except himself.

Patsy reached out for Horace, but the shameless creature, obviously knowing when he was well off, had snuggled against his new protector. Patsy smiled at them and went to strip the bed.

'That's finished me,' Nick prophesied gloomily to Derek. 'Now Katie's cooed over that smelly mothbag, Patsy's hers for life.'

'It's not your day, is it?' Derek said with a grin.

At last normality was restored. Horace was persuaded to settle into his basket, and Nick once more broached the subject of bed.

'Oh, not yet,' Katie pleaded. 'I feel so alive, I could—' The phone rang by her elbow and she picked it up. 'Hallo?'

'Is Nick there?' came a woman's voice. 'Or have I got the wrong number?'

'No, this is Nick's number. Who shall I say?'

'Tell him it's Lilian. And I suppose you must be little Katie?'

There was a touch of gritted teeth about Katie's reply. 'Yes, I'm 'little Katie'. *Nick! It's Lilian!*'

He hurried over to take the receiver. 'Lilian? Hallo, darling!' There was an unmistakable note of relief in his voice. It was so nice to talk to a woman who didn't lay traps for him, and could be relied on to stay the same from one minute to the next.

'Poor Nick. You sound frayed at the edges.'

'Yes, I am a bit. In fact, more than a bit.'

'Is she being very trying?'

'You could say that,' Nick said, with a cautious eye on Katie.

'I suppose you won't have any time for me while she's here?'

'Nonsense, I'm longing to see you. How about tomorrow night? Dinner and dancing at our usual place?'

'Sounds lovely.'

'Why don't you wear that pale blue thing I like so much?'

'Just to please you.'

He bid her an affectionate goodnight and hung up, feeling better.

Derek had opened a bottle of wine and was filling a glass for Katie.

'I won't, thank you,' she said quickly. 'I think I'll go to bed.'

'Nonsense, the night is young yet.'

'I've had a long journey.'

'Are you all right?' Nick asked. 'A moment ago you were full of beans.'

'Yes, well…' For a moment her voice trembled and her eyes were oddly bright. 'I've suddenly discovered that I'm more tired than I thought. Goodnight, everyone.'

Lilian had fair, delicate looks, and wide blue eyes with a lot of shrewdness in their depths. Her manners were calm, and being with her was calculated to soothe a suffering man. She listened to Nick's story with a smile of amused tolerance, and shook her head in sympathy.

'My poor dear! Whatever were they thinking of to dump her on you?'

'Well, I suppose it's not her fault she's twenty-one,' he conceded, large-mindedly. 'If she'd really been just a kid I could have coped better.'

'Can't Patsy take her off your hands?'

'Patsy,' he said with feeling, 'has been her slave since the first evening. She's planning to take a day off, because Katie wants to shop for new clothes and doesn't know the best places.'

'But, Nick, you must learn to be firm with this girl. She can't be allowed to turn your whole life upside down.'

'Strange. That's what I keep saying to myself. But it happens anyway. To be fair, she was all right today. I gave her a guidebook, told her to go to the Tower of London, and she went off like a lamb.' He gave a sudden laugh. 'Mind you, she's mad at me right now because I let on that I used to call her the Poison Pixie.'

Lilian gave a silvery laugh. 'Was it appropriate?'

'I thought so at the time. Though I wouldn't have said that if I'd known I was talking to her.'

'She actually deceived you into thinking she was someone else?'

'Not deliberately. I just didn't recognise her.'

'But she didn't *un*deceive you when she should have done. Don't you think that's slightly devious?'

Nick, who'd said exactly the same thing to himself at the time, now found himself protesting, 'Oh, come on. She was just enjoying the joke. She likes a good laugh, does Katie.'

'All right. Not devious. Childish?'

'In a sense,' he said, considering. 'She's eager for life in the way a child is. She still believes in it.'

'I suppose we all believe in life.'

'No, I mean she's still convinced that life can be fun.' He added apologetically, 'I suppose at twenty-one she ought to think like that. In a way I rather envy her. It might be nice to go on believing in life that way.'

Lilian gave a gentle, incredulous laugh. 'Nick, really! Adults know that life is a serious matter. That's what I've always admired about you, the fact that you know what's important.'

'I begin to wonder,' he murmured with an unconscious sigh.

'I beg your pardon?'

'Nothing. You're quite right, of course.

He was uneasily aware that he hadn't been entirely frank with Lilian. He'd told her about Katie's age, her general appearance and her maddening behaviour. But he hadn't tried to describe the perfect proportions of her dainty figure, her vivid beauty or the radiant glow of her eyes. He told himself there was no need to trouble Lilian with these details.

Lilian was a strong-minded young woman. By profession she was a lawyer, but in her spare time she worked for various charities. Nick enjoyed her company. She was intelligent, as well as being coolly attractive. They'd been a couple for the last month. Nick had taken her to his firm's dinner dance, and had received nods of approval from the hierarchy. Even in these more casual days there were some jobs in which the right wife could be an asset, and Lilian had definitely passed muster.

He enjoyed being seen with her in a place like this, where they could dine well and dance to a small orchestra playing traditional music.

'Never mind Katie,' he said now. 'I refuse to think

about her any more. I'd rather think about you. You look gorgeous.'

'Thank you, darling. I hope you notice I'm wearing your gift.' She touched the pearl pendant about her neck. It was ideal with her restrained pastel colouring.

'Let's dance,' he said, rising and taking her into his arms.

As they circled the floor he noticed some familiar faces. Greetings were exchanged. It was all very soothing and pleasant, and exactly what he needed to combat the tensions in his home.

'Have you settled the business with Beswick's?' she asked, referring to a firm she'd sent to him for financing.

'Just about. He's got to give us a little more security than he planned on, but I think we'll agree.'

'Can you speak up?' Lilian asked. 'Suddenly I can't hear properly.'

'Neither can I.' Nick rubbed his ears. 'Where on earth is all that noise coming from?'

A burst of laughter answered him, and they turned their heads to see a party entering the restaurant. There were three young men, hovering around a girl in the centre. They all seemed anxious to get her attention, and she smiled at each one by turn.

The waiter indicated a table. One of the young men took the girl's right hand, one took her left, and the third pulled out a chair.

'That seems a rather undiscriminating young woman,' Lilian observed. 'I wonder if she realises she's making a show of herself.'

'Perhaps she's a visiting film star, and those are her minders,' Nick mused. 'No, hang on, one of them's Derek. Good grief! *Katie!*'

He had a brief, clear view of her, laughing directly

into the eyes of one of her escorts. Derek intervened, claiming her attention. The third escort protested jealously. The goddess sat there, smiling benevolently on her worshippers.

'You don't mean that's Katie?' Lilian asked in a strange voice.

'Yes, it is. And there's Derek with her. I don't know who the others are. I think I'd better—'

'Don't go striding over there,' Lilian said, holding him with fingers whose possessive strength he hadn't suspected before. 'That's just pandering to her need for attention.'

'You're right. The only way to cope with Katie is to rise loftily above her.' He added with a grin, 'I just hope she doesn't shoot me down.'

It was a very mild joke, and it was unreasonable of him to be irked when Lilian didn't understand it. After all, it was the first one she'd ever heard him make.

He forgot Katie for the moment, enjoying the new mood of demonstrativeness that had come over Lilian. She'd never danced so close to him before, or slipped her arm about his neck so intimately. He was unwilling to get too close to Katie's table, sure that she'd say something cheeky about Lilian later. But Lilian herself used her clinging arm to guide him close to Katie, which he felt was very forbearing of her.

'What do you think?' he asked, when Lilian had had a chance to look Katie up and down.

'My poor dear,' she sympathised. 'Whatever are you going to do with her?'

Suddenly the music changed to a rumba. As if unaware of the attention she'd attracted, Katie got languidly to her feet and glided onto the dance floor, drawing one of the young men after her with no more than a look. Lilian drew in her breath sharply.

Nick had won the battle to replace Katie's ruined dress, and for the first time he saw what she'd bought instead. It was a creation of silk chiffon in a wine-red that shouldn't have suited her but did. It was close fitting over the bosom, and down to her hips, but there it flared into several layers that floated and glided against each other as she advanced across the floor with sinuous grace and began to move with the beat. Her golden sandals seemed impossibly high, yet she never stumbled, her intricate steps as sure-footed as a gazelle's.

Nick and Lilian left the floor, and gradually the other dancers began to back off, recognising the presence of experts. Soon Katie and her partner commanded the entire floor. They were both supreme experts, moving not flashily, but with a subtlety and finesse that riveted the attention of everyone watching. There was a faint smile on Katie's face, and her eyes were half closed in an expression of elegant aloofness that was perfect, while her glittering golden feet performed steps of impossible intricacy.

The crowd began to clap and cheer. Nick's gaze never left Katie's gliding form, and without knowing it he gave a grin of appreciation. He didn't even notice Lilian watching him, her lips pursed.

The band entered into the spirit of things, speeding up the tempo, challenging the dancers. They responded with movements that were even faster and more complex. Nick held his breath, praying for Katie not to stumble, but she was in her element, moving with perfect grace and assurance. To his enchanted eyes she seemed to shine with life and youth.

At last the dancers reached a triumphant finale,

clasped theatrically in each other's arms. The applause was deafening. Nick felt as though he were coming out of a dream. He began to clap, and after a moment Lilian did so too. 'She looked charming,' she said coolly. 'But I hope exhibition dancing doesn't become the norm here. What would you and I do?'

'Follow in their footsteps?' he suggested frivolously. 'We might do worse.'

'I hope your boss never hears you saying things like that.'

'We'd better go and say hallo.' He took Lilian's hand and went across to Katie's table. She was seated, gasping slightly, her skin glowing. There were introductions all round, and Derek pulled a couple of chairs away from the next table so that Nick and Lilian could join them.

Katie was eyeing Nick askance. 'Go on, tell me off,' she challenged.

'Stop trying to make me out an ogre. I thought you were great. But what are you doing with this bad character?' He indicated Derek.

'He offered to escort me to the Tower of London. Wasn't that nice of him?'

'Yes, wasn't it? I hope he wasn't bored.'

'Well, we didn't actually go to the Tower,' Katie admitted. 'Derek showed me where he works, and we met some friends of his, and—here we all are.'

Derek's face was as bland and innocent as a baby's.

'I must tell you how much I enjoyed your charming little display,' Lilian said kindly to Katie. 'It was almost good enough to be professional.'

Derek gave a shout of laughter, which made Lilian regard him coolly. One of her virtues, in Nick's eyes, was that she was blind to Derek's charm.

'Katie *is* a professional,' Derek explained. 'So's Mac.' He indicated the young man who'd been her partner.

'A professional dancer?' Nick echoed, frowning.

'I got together with two other girls and two lads in Australia,' Katie said. 'We worked up a little act and got bookings in clubs wherever we could. It was fun while it lasted. But two of the others married each other and started a family. And my partner married a girl back home and went to work in an office. So that was that!'

A waiter appeared with a drinks tray. Under cover of the hubbub, Katie eased herself closer to Nick and asked, 'Are you sure you're not mad at me?'

'Of course not.'

'Prove it by dancing with me.'

'As long as it's a nice, sedate waltz.'

'Promise.'

'Then I'd love to.'

She was light as thistledown in his arms, and he felt almost as though he was floating with her.

'You dance wonderfully,' he said, meaning it.

'That's nice of you, but actually I'm out of condition. Mac knows a studio where I can go to some classes. I've got to be fighting fit before I can get back to work.'

A chill hand of foreboding, familiar from years before, took hold of his stomach. 'Work? You mean dancing?'

'Only in a small way. I'm not going on the stage, or anything. Just a little cabaret turn for clubs, posh restaurants, private functions and so on.'

'I doubt there's much cabaret work to be had in Delford.'

'Really?'

'I think it's only got one nightclub. It's not like London up there, you know.'

'I'm so glad I talked to you about it,' Katie said eagerly. 'I knew you'd give me good advice.'

'I didn't want to see you make a mistake.'

She beamed at him. 'London it is, then.'

'What?'

'I'm going to stay here. Ouch! That was my foot!'

'Katie, you can't stay here!'

'But it was your idea.'

'It certainly wasn't.'

'You were the one who mentioned London.'

'But not— Hell, Katie! You know what I meant.'

'I don't think I do. One minute you're saying that London's the only place for what I want to do—which it is. The next moment you're trying to throw me out.'

'Stop making a drama out of this. Nobody's throwing you out.'

'You didn't want me in the first place.'

He groaned. 'Are we going over that again?'

'No. The sooner I leave your flat the better.'

'You're not leaving. What would Isobel say?'

'She'll understand when I tell her everything.'

Well-founded fear of Katie's version of 'everything' made him say firmly, 'You'll do no such thing, you scheming little minx. You'll stay in my home so that I can keep an eye on you.'

'But if I'm going to be *crushed* by the burden of your disapproval—'

Against his will, Nick started to grin. 'Cut it out, Katie. I've disapproved of you since the day we met. You've never been crushed before. Me, yes. You, never.'

She gazed up at him sunnily. 'That's settled, then.'

Suddenly he burst out laughing. He couldn't help it. She joined him, giggling like a conspirator. Heads turned in their direction. Lilian raised her eyebrows and her mouth tightened very slightly.

'You wretch!' Nick said with feeling.

'You don't mind me, really, do you, Nick?'

'Do I get a choice?'

'Nope!'

They laughed again. Then he said, 'But it's still not a good idea, Katie. I don't want to see you end up exhausted, disillusioned and hurt.'

'Why must you look on the gloomy side?'

He looked at her, thinking how frail and delicate she seemed for the hard slog she was planning. She floated like gossamer, and, although it was a delightful feeling, it filled him with fear for her. But he said none of this, knowing it would only incite her to tease him.

'Because the gloomy side is usually the right one,' he said simply.

'Not always. Just suppose some nightclub impresario had been here tonight, and he'd seen Mac and me dancing and swept us off to sign a contract.'

'That only happens in films, not in real life.'

'But it might. Can't you see that's what's so wonderful? Anything might happen. You could get your heart's desire even when it seems impossible. You have to believe in that chance, or there'd be no point in being alive.'

And she was very much alive, he thought. Beautifully, gloriously alive, in the way fire was alive, and the stars were alive.

'What are you smiling at?' she asked.

'Was I smiling? I was just thinking how young you are.'

'Not really. You're used to thinking of me as a child, but I'm a fully grown woman now.'

'All five foot three of you?' he teased.

She chuckled. 'For me, that *is* fully grown. I'm a woman, Nick. I know what I want, and I have to believe I'm going to get it, or—' She broke off suddenly, and he had the feeling that she was looking at some beautiful inner vision, tinged with sadness.

'Or what?' he asked gently. 'What will you do if you don't get your heart's desire?'

'I'll get it. I couldn't have worked and prayed and dreamed this long, all for nothing.'

'Dancing really means that much?'

'Dancing? Oh, yes, dancing.'

'Well, that was what we were talking about, wasn't it?'

'Yes—yes, of course.'

'I hope you get everything you want, Katie,' he said tenderly.

'I will. I must,' she said, with an intensity that startled him.

'Try not to get hurt, my dear,' he said gently. 'I know what it feels like to yearn for something that means more to you than everything else in the world and still not get it.'

'You mean Isobel, don't you?' she asked, her face clouded.

'Yes.'

'But you didn't win her because she wasn't right for you. Oh, Nick, you mustn't be in love with her now.'

'Mustn't I? I can't help it if she's still there in my heart. I guess she always will be. Let's not talk about it.'

He waltzed her back to the table, but Katie wouldn't sit down. 'I must go and powder my nose,' she said, and floated away.

'I want a word with you,' Nick said to Derek. 'Do you know what you've started? Katie's going to work up another act.'

'And that's my fault?'

'You introduced her to that fellow.'

'Don't worry about Katie. She's got her head screwed on right. I showed her my office today, explained all about my business, and she followed everything I said. Apparently her father made her take a computer course before she went off with this act.'

'Well, that's a relief.' He looked around. 'Where's Lilian?'

'She seems to have vanished.'

Katie was checking her lipstick in the mirror when Lilian glided into the rest room. She smiled and settled down into one of the luxurious armchairs.

'I'm surprised you aren't putting your feet up for a few minutes,' she said. 'That dance must really have taken it out of you.'

'I could dance all night,' Katie assured her.

'I must say, you're not a bit the way Nick led me to believe. It's too bad of him.'

'What—did Nick say about me?' Katie asked casually.

'Oh, nothing, really. I think he got a bit carried away. Now I've met you, I can see that you're very charming.'

'But Nick didn't tell you I was charming?'

'My dear, I discounted most of it. I think he was in a bad mood. Poison Pixie, indeed! I thought that was going too far.'

'Much too far,' Katie said lightly.

If she was displeased, nothing showed in her manner when she returned to the table. She laughed and teased her three cavaliers so cheerfully that Nick left her with an easy mind, after warning Derek about taking her home.

When he reached his flat later, after dropping Lilian at her elegant apartment, he found Patsy watching television, alone.

'No sign of the delinquents?' he asked.

'Oh, yes, they've been back an hour. Derek's working in his room, and Katie went to bed with a headache.'

'I'm not surprised. She really danced up a storm.' He described the evening's events to Patsy, who nodded thoughtfully.

'What did Lilian think of Katie?'

'She didn't take to her at first,' Nick admitted. 'But they had a natter in the ladies' rest room, and Lilian came out smiling. They're going to be friends.'

'Oh, really?' Patsy echoed, with something in her voice that worried him. 'Did Katie come out smiling?'

'I suppose so. She seemed cheerful enough. I didn't notice much. I can't spend my whole life thinking about Katie.'

'Keep your voice down.' She shushed him, with a warning look at Katie's door.

'My voice wasn't up,' he protested.

'Your voice rises whenever you get agitated, and you get agitated when you talk about Katie. So Lilian's fine about her? She didn't say anything afterwards?'

Nick shrugged. 'She never mentioned Katie's name for the rest of the evening.'

'Hmm!' Again her voice held that strange note.

'Patsy,' he said patiently, 'am I missing something here?'

'You certainly are, but if I explained it to you you'd still miss it. So let's drop the subject.'

The phone saved him from having to answer. The man's voice on the other end was deep and had an Australian accent.

'I've heard Katie's there. Is that right?'

'Who is this?'

'Jake Ratchett. I want to speak to Katie.'

'Hold on. I'm not sure Katie wants to speak to you.'

'Look, I've come halfway around the world to find her, and I'm not just going to hang up.'

'Halfway—? You mean you're here, in England?'

'I sure am. Now where is she?'

'Well, Mr Ratchett, you've got a damned cheek!' Nick exclaimed. He disliked everything about this man, especially the possessive way he talked about Katie.

'Never mind me. I want to talk to her.'

Katie's bedroom door opened and she slipped out, wearing a light dressing gown. Her make-up was gone, and she looked very young and rather strained. 'I'll talk to him,' she said, reaching for the phone. But Nick held onto it.

'This man's followed you to England, and he sounds an ugly customer. I think you should leave him to me.'

'I can cope with Jake. Hallo, Jake? Nick says you're in England—you shouldn't have come all this way—yes, I know, but I told you—Jake, please—I tried to explain—no, I don't think that's a good idea. Maybe you should just go back home—'

Nick couldn't stand it any longer. Seizing the receiver from her, he spoke into it sternly. 'Listen to me, Ratchett. Katie doesn't want to see you, and that's enough. If you bother her again, you'll have me to deal with.' He slammed down the phone.

Katie's face didn't suggest that she was overwhelmed by this display of knight errantry.

'That was very high-handed,' she said coolly.

'He was pestering you. I got rid of him.'

'Did I ask you to? I can cope with Jake.'

'I don't think you can. He sounded a very nasty piece of work, and if he's followed you over here, he means business.'

She sighed. 'I'm going back to bed.'

'And that's all the thanks I get? Why are you scowling at me?'

The look she flung at him could only be described as withering. 'You really don't know, do you?'

'Because I took the phone?'

'No, I forgive you for that.'

'Forgi—? Give me patience, somebody!'

'What I can't forgive is you telling Lilian something that was private between us.'

'Nothing's private between us,' he said, baffled.

'But it should have been. How dare you tell her about Poison Pixie? That's private!'

'I told *Jennifer* about it too, don't forget.'

'That was me.'

'But I didn't know.'

'I don't care. It's not the same.'

'Katie, I'm lost here. I honestly don't know what you're in such a temper about.'

'No, you don't, do you?' she said stormily. 'If you had the slightest sensitivity you would have. But you haven't. So you don't.'

'Katie—!'

'I'm going to bed, Nick. I don't want to discuss this any further.' She retreated into her room.

Nick was left staring at her closed door. A glance at Patsy's face failed to enlighten him. He appealed to her, to the door, to the heavens.

'What did I do? *What the blue blazes did I do?*'

CHAPTER FOUR

'YOU'LL wear the clock face out if you keep looking at it like that,' Patsy observed.

'It's nearly two in the morning,' Nick said, unnecessarily.

'I know that.'

'And they're not in yet.'

'You only got home twenty minutes ago yourself,' Patsy pointed out.

'That's different. It makes me uneasy to see her going out with Derek.'

'Katie's young. It's her first trip to London.'

'And she was out three times last week,' Nick recalled gloomily.

'But not with Derek.'

'No. There was the photographer who was "looking her over" for some publicity shots, and one was a weirdo who trained *racing gerbils*. He wanted me to arrange financing for him, would you believe?'

Patsy chuckled. 'Did you see Katie's face when she realised he'd only made up to her as a way of approaching you?'

'She was as mad as a wet hen,' Nick said, grinning. 'I remember what she said to him, too. He won't be back here in a hurry. Not that she'll notice the loss among so many. And she went out with Mac, the dancing partner, to "make plans". I thought he was a nasty piece of work, but Katie says they make beautiful music together. Plus a date with Derek.'

'She really knows how to enjoy herself, doesn't she?' Patsy said cheerfully.

'She knows how to turn my hair white.'

'Nick, if you don't like Katie's choice of men-friends, you should take her out yourself, like Isobel wanted.'

'How would I explain to Lilian? I suppose I could always take them both out together...'

'Not if you want to live,' Patsy warned.

'You're right,' Nick said with a shudder.

He went to his room to take off his jacket. When he returned there was still no sign of the delinquents. Patsy thrust a mug of cocoa into his hand. It was years since he'd drunk anything so childish, but it was delicious.

'Stop fretting,' she commanded.

'I'm not fretting. Why should I fret? She can take care of herself, so she keeps telling me.'

'Then believe her. That is one very confident young woman.'

'If you mean that she knows how to get the whole world doing her bidding, regardless of anyone else's convenience, I agree,' he said significantly.

'Nick, really! Just because I took one day off to help her shop for clothes! It was the least I could do after Horace's slip-up.'

'That's another thing. Horace! He's always hated everyone on principle, but he adores Katie.'

'Everyone adores Katie, except you,' Patsy told him severely. 'You're turning into a miserable curmudgeon.'

Before he could answer there came a muffled explosion of laughter outside the front door.

'They're back,' Patsy said.

The laughter was followed by a long silence, which had Nick's fevered imagination working overtime. Obviously Derek was kissing her, and Katie, poor deluded girl, had fallen, helpless, into his clutches. The silence stretched on and on, and Nick ground his nails into his palm.

'When they come in, don't let her see that you're upset,' Patsy murmured.

'I'm not upset,' he said quickly.

At last he heard the front door open and close very gently, the sound of whispers and more laughter. Then another silence, broken only by a soft 'Mmm' from Katie.

This was disgraceful, and Nick's duty was clear. He switched on the hall light, and the two in each other's arms jumped guiltily apart. They looked as if they'd been somewhere formal. Derek actually wore a dress shirt, with embroidery and ruffles down the front, and Katie was dressed in a floating green creation that looked ravishing on her.

'Do you know what hour this is?' Nick asked grimly.

'It's two in the morning,' Katie said, all innocence.

'And you think this is a suitable time to come in?'

'Stop acting like a Victorian Papa,' Derek told him provocatively. 'Katie's been perfectly safe with me.'

'Is *any* woman safe with you?' Nick demanded.

'Katie, have you been safe?' Derek asked.

'Yes, I have,' she said in an injured tone. 'And I want to know why? What's wrong with me?'

'Not a thing,' he assured her. 'Besides, I kissed you.'

'One measly little kiss—'

'Two,' Nick growled.

'Two measly little kisses are hardly the dangerous seduction I was led to expect,' she complained.

'Did you want him to seduce you?' Nick asked, outraged.

'I expected him to jolly well try,' she said indignantly.

'He did try,' Nick snapped. 'I heard you, both times.'

'Phooey!' she said. 'You don't call that trying, do you?'

'All right, let's have another go,' Derek said, seizing her dramatically and turning her so that she leaned back across his arm. Katie giggled and embraced him back, with little murmuring sounds of appreciation. Nick ground his teeth.

'They make such a picture together,' Patsy cooed, smiling. 'Doesn't it make you feel good just to look at them?'

'No, it doesn't,' Nick snapped.

He was in an unenviable position. Responsible for Katie, yet with no authority to curb her crazy behaviour. It would end in tears and he would get the blame.

At last the lovers disentangled themselves. Katie, Nick observed, was regarding him with eyes full of wicked mischief. 'Stop trying to wind me up,' he told her severely. 'I've learned to rise above you.'

'Oh, Nick, was that very hard?' Katie asked, awed.

'I'm working at it. Now I'm going to bed. Goodnight.'

Derek and Katie continued to spend a lot of time together, but to Nick's relief Derek was leaving soon on a trip to promote his latest products, and would be away several weeks. The day he departed Katie registered with the same dance studio that Mac attended, and after that she went to a class there every morning.

'Can you afford it?' Nick asked, glancing at the list of prices. 'This place isn't cheap.'

'I know. I'm going to get a job to pay my fees, and give you some for my keep.'

'Cut that out!'

'No, really. I don't expect to live here rent-free.'

'What would Isobel say if I accepted money from you? It's out of the question.'

Katie didn't reply, and all his alarm bells rang. He'd already learned that when Katie stopped arguing it meant that she was simply going to ignore him.

'Patsy, you're not to take a penny from her,' he said quickly. 'If you need more housekeeping money, just tell me. Katie, I'm serious about this. I hope you're both listening.'

'Yes, *sir*!' they chimed in chorus, saluting smartly.

'Very funny, both of you.'

He thought himself inured to Katie by this time, but, even so, nothing had prepared him for the evening she returned home announcing that she had a job at the Pop-Eyed Parrot.

'Don't get worked up about this,' Patsy warned him.

'Don't get worked up! She's going to work in a sleazy dive—'

'It's a nightclub,' Katie said defiantly.

'And I'll bet I know what kind of nightclub,' Nick said darkly.

'You'd be wrong,' Patsy assured him. 'I've been there, and it's very respectable.'

'Patsy, I appreciate that you're always on Katie's side, but that's going too far. You don't haunt niteries.'

'You know very little,' Patsy told him firmly. 'I have a gentleman friend who likes to entertain me to an evening out occasionally. He took me to the Pop-Eyed Parrot last month, and I didn't see anything that offended me.'

'What did the waitresses wear?' Nick demanded suspiciously.

'It's a sort of bathing costume—quite modestly cut

for these days—with feathers. And they work terribly hard. You'll be run off your feet, Katie.'

'She won't, because she's not going to work in a nightclub, no matter how respectable it is,' Nick said firmly. 'Good grief! What would Isobel say?'

'Don't worry,' Katie said kindly. 'You can tell Isobel that you forbade me in the strongest possible terms, and I took no notice whatever. After all, that's what's going to happen.'

She couldn't be budged from this position. Nick fell back on seeking Isobel's help, but, although concerned, she agreed that there was nothing he could do.

'I know you did your best, Nick, dear,' she said warmly. 'But Katie's headstrong. Just keep a very close eye on her. You know, drop in and see what sort of place it is.'

'I'll certainly do that,' he said grimly. He came off the phone to find Katie vanished and Patsy eyeing him sympathetically.

'How are you going to explain to Isobel that you haven't kept your word?' she asked.

'How have I broken my word? I spend most of my waking life thinking about Katie, worrying about—'

'But you don't take her out, the way you said you would. And when she's working at this place she won't have many free evenings. So you'd better get moving.'

He couldn't deny the good sense of this, and when Katie emerged he poured her a cup of tea and suggested an outing. 'That is, if you can find time for me in your crowded schedule, Miss Deakins?'

She pretended to consider. 'I dare say I can squeeze you in, Mr Kenton. If you're really set on taking me out.'

'Well, as Patsy has pointed out to me, I promised

Isobel that I'd escort you sometimes, and so far I've neglected that duty.'

'Thanks a lot,' Katie said indignantly. 'You really know how to deliver an irresistible invitation, Nick.'

'Tomorrow evening, at seven, at the Cottage Pie. It's a little pub near the river. I've got to meet someone there for a drink, but it won't take long, and then we'll go for a meal.'

He'd planned to be finished with his duty drink by the time Katie arrived, but his client lingered. He began to get nervous. The thought of her intruding her boisterous presence into a delicately balanced discussion made him flinch, and when he saw her come in he crossed his fingers. But she took in the situation and sat down quietly, where he couldn't see her even out of the corner of his eye.

The meeting dragged on and on. Every time Nick thought they were through, the client remembered something else. It was a full two hours before he was free, and he groaned inwardly at what Katie would say to him. But he found her all smiles and good temper. She'd fallen into conversation with an elderly man, and seemed perfectly content.

'I'm sorry, Katie,' Nick said when he had her to himself. 'I feel terrible, treating you like that.'

'It couldn't be helped. He was important to you, wasn't he?'

'Very. I've been trying to get him into my office for ages, then yesterday he calls up and says let's meet for one "very quick drink". You're a most forgiving person.'

'What did you expect?' she said with a smile. 'That I was going to throw a childish tantrum?'

He reddened, but disclaimed hastily, 'I wouldn't have blamed you for being a bit annoyed.'

'I was. I could have cheerfully strangled that man. But showing it is another matter.'

It flashed through his mind that Lilian would also have been gracious in these circumstances, but she would have added a few pointed remarks about poor organisation.

'Let me feed you quickly, to make amends.'

'What a perfect thing to say. *I* may not be complaining, but my stomach is throwing a fit of temper.'

'They've got a good restaurant here—'

'Oh, no, let's escape before he decides to come back,' she said hastily.

'You're right.'

Dusk had fallen as they walked down by the Thames, watching the lights winking in the ripples. Boats chugged by, sounding their horns to each other.

'This is beautiful,' Katie sighed, leaning on the parapet and looking out over the water with shining eyes. 'Oh, Nick, look! Over there. That boat is a restaurant.'

'Come on,' he said, taking her hand and starting to run.

Two crew members of the *Marianne* were just about to cast off, but they waited for them.

'Just in time, sir,' the Chief Steward said as they raced down the gangplank. 'Table for two?'

'Can we sit by the window?' Katie begged.

'I'm afraid those tables fill up first—' the Steward began, but stopped as he felt the note Nick was slipping into his hand. 'But we'll see what we can do.'

Nick wondered what had got into him. Bribery was against his principles. But disappointing Katie was also against his principles, he'd just discovered.

The steward led them to a small table that was being hastily set up by a large window. The small, flickering candles offered just enough light to read the menus, but not enough to spoil the view out over the river. The boat began to chug gently away from the pier.

Katie occupied the first few minutes studying the menu and choosing everything that was most fattening.

'You want to be careful,' Nick warned. 'You may not gain weight now, but it'll all catch up with you in a few years.'

'No, it won't,' she said with sunny self-confidence.

'Think you can make everything work out as you want, huh?' he asked, amused. 'The annoying thing is, *you* usually can.'

'Not everything, Nick. There's something I want terribly, but I'm no nearer getting it than I was years ago.'

'Tell me about it.'

'Not now. I'll tell you one day—if—if things work out.' Seeing him about to ask another question, she quickly changed the subject. 'Anyway, eating anything I like is mostly a con, because I'll actually work all this off dancing.'

She shrugged off her linen jacket, revealing a pretty white silk top against which nestled a pendant with a single glittering stone.

She saw him looking, and patted the pendant. 'It's pretty, isn't it?'

'Very,' Nick said. 'Did you buy it in Australia?'

'Did I—? You gave it to me.'

'No way,' he said with a grin. 'Don't tell me I bought you presents. We never ceased hostilities long enough.'

'You gave it to me when Isobel married, to wear with my bridesmaid's dress.'

He was about to deny it when the memory came back to him.

'That's right, I did. The best man is supposed to give

the bridesmaid a gift. At least, that's what Isobel told me.'

'And of course we were still at daggers drawn,' Katie said. 'Did you mind very much having to buy your enemy a present?'

'I didn't really. Isobel chose it, and I just paid. I never even saw it until you opened the box.'

'Oh,' she said softly.

'It made sense that way. Isobel knew what you needed and I didn't.'

'Yes, of course,' Katie said in the same tone. But Nick was pouring her a glass of wine, and didn't notice the wistful look on her face.

'Katie, this Ratchett character worries me. Tell me some more about him.'

'Have you ever heard of Ekton, Ratchett & Proud?'

'One of the biggest industrial groups in the world? Of course. You don't mean he comes from that family?'

'His father is *the* Ratchett. He put a lot of business Dad's way, and invited us to his home for a weekend. That's how I met Jake.'

'Good grief!' he said faintly. 'If you play your cards right you could be a multi-millionairess.'

'Nick, it isn't funny. I don't fancy Jake, but I can't make him understand that I mean it.'

'You're right, it isn't funny. He's probably never been denied anything in his life.'

'Still, I never thought he'd follow me all this way.'

'I'm surprised he hasn't turned up on the doorstep.'

'He's clever. Flowers and phone calls to soften me up. Then he'll appear, and I'll end up going out with him so as not to seem rude.'

'If he dares to show his face I'll deal with him.'

'Oh, Nick, be careful, please. I have to think of Dad. He needs their business.'

'But it's intolerable of your father to put you in this position.'

'Dad doesn't know. If he did, it would put *him* in an awful position. I thought leaving Australia would solve the problem. But it seems not. Anyway,' she added airily, 'I wanted to come home and see how the Old Country had managed without me.'

'The Old Country is still reeling from the shock,' he assured her. 'So am I.'

'You'll recover,' she said cheerfully. 'Eventually.'

'"Eventually" is a long way off. I've got grey hairs that I didn't have before you arrived. You've no idea of time, you're hopelessly disorganised, you're late, you're untidy.'

'That's not fair,' she protested. 'I worked ever so hard to straighten up the flat the other day.'

'I know. I still can't find half my stuff. My bureau is packed with lonely socks, pining for their lost mates.'

'I only *tidied* it.'

'It didn't need tidying until you'd done your worst.'

Katie sniffed. 'You're very unkind to me, Nick—'

'And you can stop that. I know you too well by now.'

She beamed. 'Bet you don't. Bet you don't know me at all.'

'Bet I do,' he said, before he could stop himself. 'You never cry, not really. You're the sunniest-tempered person I know. It's one of the things I like about you.'

'You mean you actually *like* things about me? Oh, do tell me about the others.'

'There aren't any others,' he said, retrieving ground quickly. 'You're a horror.'

'But you said—'

'I was being polite.'

'You?'

'Finish what you're eating,' he said with a grin. 'They want to serve the next course.'

They chatted cheerfully for the rest of the meal.

Katie's merry disposition made her a pleasant companion. Nick actually ventured one of his rare jokes, and she laughed aloud in instant comprehension. He didn't make jokes with Lilian. She always looked puzzled and said, 'Whatever do you mean?' And when he tried to explain, the joke simply fell to pieces.

Encouraged, he ventured another witticism, and Katie said triumphantly, 'You see? You're not such a stick-in-the-mud as you pretend.'

By now he had her measure, and merely laughed as he said, 'Thank you, kind lady.'

He had a disconcerting feeling of having lived through this moment before. He'd had it once previously, when they'd met at the railway station that first day, an inexplicable conviction that Katie and Isobel had something mysterious in common. It was like being haunted by the ghost of someone who was actually sitting there with you, and it made no sense.

'What's up?' Katie asked.

'Nothing,' he said hastily, shaking his head. If she knew his fanciful thoughts he reckoned she would have a field day, teasing him.

They finished the meal in charity with one another. It lasted until they were halfway home. But then Nick ruined everything by trying again to warn her off the Pop-Eyed Parrot. Katie refused to budge. He became annoyed. Words were said. They were largely a re-run of the previous day's argument, but with added heat. By the time they reached home they were no longer talking.

Patsy, who'd gone to bed an hour ago, put her head around her bedroom door long enough to see them bid each other a frigid goodnight and retire. She gave an exasperated sigh, and rolled her eyes to heaven.

She maintained a tactful silence the next morning, but contrived, in her own way, to let Nick know that she was cross with him. In the early hours of the morning she'd come to a decision, and was debating the best way to put it into practise.

They drove separately to work. Nick would have gladly given her a lift, but Patsy insisted on the independence of her own car. She got in just ahead of him, and had freshly perked coffee waiting when he arrived.

'Bless you, Patsy,' he said, giving her his most charming smile. 'The coffee's splendid, as always.'

'Stop trying to get round me,' she said severely. 'I heard you last night, being unkind to poor Katie.'

'How about "poor Nick"?'

'Phooey!'

'Take a month's notice, Mrs Cornell.'

'Certainly, sir. Do I add that to last week's month's notice, or the one you gave me for saying it wasn't Katie's fault you'd lost your favourite tie?'

'OK, OK, I'm sorry. It's just that between you and the Poison Pixie I'm feeling a bit bruised.'

'Then you'll be glad to know that I'm leaving.'

'Hey, I didn't mean it about the month's notice.'

'No, I mean leaving the flat.'

He paled. 'You can't desert me now.'

'I'm afraid I have to. Jack, my younger boy, is begging me to go and stay with him for a while. He's had another big row with his wife and he needs me to keep the peace.'

'*I* need you to keep the peace.'

'Not as much as he does. I'll still be at work every day, but if I'm at his house in the evenings I can look after the children and give him and Brenda some time to sort themselves out.'

He knew it wasn't worth arguing. Patsy wore her implacable look. He wrote her a generous cheque, which Patsy pocketed with a smile. 'Barbados, here I come,' she said.

He had to leave immediately for a meeting. Patsy waited until he'd safely gone before picking up the phone and dialling.

'Brenda, darling, how would you like to invite your favourite mother-in-law for a visit? Good! I'll arrive this evening. We won't tell Jack. Let it come as a big surprise!'

CHAPTER FIVE

NICK had to admit that at first glance the Pop-Eyed Parrot was fairly reassuring. It had an elegant entrance in a well-lit street, with a uniformed doorman who tipped his hat. So far, so good.

The size of the entrance fee made him gulp, but he supposed it was worth the money to know that Katie was in a decent place. A man in white tie and tails signed him in and led him down a long staircase decorated as a jungle fantasy. The walls looked like a mass of tree trunks, and thick foliage hung overhead. Animal sounds reached him as if from a distance. Parrots appeared and disappeared among the greenery, and it took him a moment to realise that they were holograms.

'All the latest that science has to offer for our customers' pleasure,' his escort intoned when he mentioned this. 'If you'll just follow me through here, sir.'

He led the way to a bamboo curtain and drew it aside for Nick to pass through. His manner plainly indicated that he expected a large tip for this small service. Nick complied with an inner groan.

Once inside, he had to stop while his eyes grew accustomed to the dim lighting. At last he could see the tables that were arranged around a cabaret floor, and immediately recognised a man he knew, dining with his wife. There was a fair spattering of middle-aged women, and Nick began to relax.

He'd taken the precaution of wearing a dinner jacket,

and was glad of it when he saw how the other diners were dressed.

Young women flitted about bearing trays of drinks. They all wore costumes that looked like one-piece bathing suits in brilliant red, yellow, green or blue satin, dotted with sequins. Their behinds were adorned with glittering feathers, and more feathers danced on their heads.

The male staff were dressed like waiters, except that they too were in parrot colours. An acid-green man conducted him to a table by the wall. It, too, was part of the jungle fantasy, with trailing greenery and a small lamp masquerading as a pineapple. A hologram parrot disconcerted him by appearing and disappearing at the corner of his eye.

'Your wine hostess will be with you in a moment,' the waiter said, and backed away.

Nick had time to look around at the girls as they dodged through the narrow spaces between the tables. From their fixed smiles, he guessed they were struggling with boredom, and, if their high heels were anything to go by, painful feet.

Poor Katie! he thought. *It's not as bad as I feared, but I'm still not leaving you here.*

The thought of Katie in that costume, her lovely figure studied by a thousand male eyes, revolted him. This place could be as respectable as it liked. It wasn't good enough for his Katie—*Isobel's* Katie, he corrected himself hastily.

A yellow parrot tripped towards him, her sequins winking in the multi-coloured lights.

'Can I take your—? *Nick!* What are you doing here?'

'Surprised? You must have known I'd want to see

where you're working. Sit down, Katie, and talk to me properly.'

'I can't. I have only half a minute to take your order.'

'I'm not staying here, I'm taking you home. Go and get changed.'

Katie's smile became brighter than ever. 'The champagne is very good, sir...'

'I don't want champagne,' he said firmly. 'I want you to do as I say, right now.'

In his agitation he reached out for her, but she backed off, saying *No!* fiercely. Nick reddened, shocked at the way she'd recoiled from his touch, and she hastened to say, 'I'm thinking of you. I don't want the bouncers to throw you out.'

'Bouncers?' he echoed, appalled.

She indicated two men, dressed as waiters in scarlet and kingfisher-blue, watching them closely.

'You'd better order something quickly,' she whispered.

'I'm blowed if I will. I want you out of here.'

The bouncers strolled over casually. 'Any trouble, Katie?' one of them asked.

'None,' she said at once. 'The customer was just ordering champagne.'

'Well done!'

Nick understood that remark when she brought the champagne and he saw the bill.

'For one bottle!' he said hoarsely.

'This is one of London's premier nightspots,' Katie recited, deadpan. 'The price is standard for the venue.'

'Stop talking gobbledegook,' he snapped.

'If it makes you feel any better, I get commission.'

'It doesn't. It's robbery.'

'Not until you've paid for it. I'm supposed to collect the money now.'

Groaning, he took out his credit card. 'Take this, then sit down and talk to me,' he said through gritted teeth.

'Certainly, sir. For a bottle of champagne, the wine hostess can sit at your table for ten minutes.'

'All right. I can say all I have to in ten minutes.'

She sashayed smartly away. Watching her, Nick had to admit that she could wear the outrageous costume with elegance and dash. In fact she outshone all the others, especially in the way she coped with the suicidally high heels.

She was back in a moment, perching on the side of the chair, crossing her beautiful silken legs. 'What would sir like to talk about?'

'Sir would like to talk about what you think you're up to.'

She opened the bottle expertly, and poured him a glass. 'I told you, I'm going to support myself.'

'Like this?' he demanded, sipping tentatively and making a disgusted face. 'Surely you can find something better?'

'Doing what? I'm not one of the world's mighty intellectuals. This is something I can do.'

'I should think conning people into buying overpriced champagne is something anyone can do.'

'Oh, no, they can't. Lilian would make a mess of it, for one.'

'Lilian wouldn't even try.'

'Very wise of her. She hasn't got the legs for it.'

'There's nothing wrong with Lilian's legs,' he said, stung. 'Anyway, how do you know? You've never seen her legs.'

'I saw the lower half of them on the night we met, and she's got thick ankles.'

'She most certainly has not.'

'When did you last look at them?'

'Katie, I am not going to sit here discussing Lilian's ankles.'

'You started it.'

'I—? May you be forgiven! I never—'

'You sneered at my job. I merely pointed out that it takes specialised skills, which Lilian doesn't have.'

'We won't discuss that,' he said firmly.

'All right, if you're sensitive about her ankles—'

'For the last time, Lilian does not have thick ankles!' he roared.

The frightful silence that greeted this explosion made him look around in horror. Everyone was staring at him, which was all Katie's fault. He'd never got into these situations before she arrived.

'I don't want you working here,' he said through gritted teeth.

'I can take care of myself.'

'A girl who could take care of herself would never end up dressed like a badly wrapped Christmas present.'

'How dare you?' she said in outrage. 'I'm nothing of the kind.'

'That's what you look like to me.'

'If you can't tell a parrot when you see one—'

'Well, pardon my ignorance,' he said with awful sarcasm. 'You're just the first parrot I've ever seen in six-inch heels, touting cheap champagne at vintage prices.'

'That is your misfortune,' she said glacially.

'Parrot indeed!'

Katie became very angry. 'Nick, I am a parrot. Is that

clear? We're all dressed in parrot colours and parrot feathers. I happened to draw yellow. I look like a parrot.'

'You look like a feather duster.'

'I am a parrot!' she said furiously. 'To any man with eyes in his head it's perfectly obvious that *I am a parrot*.'

'It's perfectly obvious that you've taken leave of your senses,' he growled. 'This nonsense ends here. Please get your clothes; we're leaving.'

'Stop talking like my father. I'm twenty-one, and I'll go home when I'm ready.'

'Katie, I mean it.'

'So do I.'

She rose from the table. Forgetting caution, he grabbed hold of her. What happened then was too fast to follow. The red and blue waiters appeared from nowhere, detached him from Katie, and the next thing he knew he was outside the club, wondering what had happened. It had taken exactly twenty seconds.

He drove home, bitterly castigating himself. What a blind fool he'd been to think she'd changed! She was still the Poison Pixie. None of her past antics had been as bad as this, but it was no more than he should have expected.

It was his own fault for having a trusting nature. To think he'd been worried about her, had wanted to protect her! Well, he knew better now. She would reach home to find her packed bags in the middle of the floor and a curt note from himself telling her to leave.

In the end he baulked at doing her packing, but he was resolved on the curt note. He was still trying to get the wording right two hours later, when she burst in.

'Oh, Nick,' she said contritely, 'I'm so sorry.'

The next moment she hurtled across the floor and

flung her arms about his neck. His offended dignity vanished and he found himself patting her back and murmuring words of consolation.

'It's all right, Katie…'

'It's not, it's not. How could I do that to you when you've been so wonderful to me? I'll never forgive myself. I wouldn't blame you if you ordered me out of your home—'

'Of course I'm not going to order you out,' he said, freeing one hand in order to screw up the note out of sight, and trying not to strangle under her embrace.

'You're so nice,' she said passionately. 'How can you be nice to me when I was rotten to you?'

'I—' He was lost for words. Her self-condemnation made him feel like a cheapskate. He put his arms about her, trying to remember that he was *in loco parentis*. Suddenly it was harder than usual. The warmth of her body pressed against his was delightful, and her hair was softly tickling his cheek. 'It wasn't so bad,' he said awkwardly.

'Did they throw you out onto the hard pavement? Are you badly hurt?'

He managed to laugh. 'Of course not. They didn't throw me anywhere, just escorted me to the door and told me to leave.'

She released his neck and stared. 'Is that all? I've been picturing you with broken bones.'

'Well, my bones aren't broken. Are you disappointed?'

'Of course not. I'd hate you to be hurt, Nick, even after the way you spoke to me.'

'Did I say anything so very terrible?'

'You said I looked like a Christmas present.'

'Well—'

'A badly wrapped Christmas present,' she said tragically. 'And a feather duster.'

He roared with laughter. 'I'm sorry, Katie. I should have seen at once that you were a parrot.' She joined in his laughter, and he asked, 'Friends again?'

'Friends,' she assured him.

'Of course we are. Always. Anyway, it's all over now, so we can forget the Pop-Eyed Parrot. Come on, admit it. Secretly you're glad to leave the place.'

'Leave?' She backed away, frowning.

'Well, you have left, haven't you?'

'Why should I?'

'How can you stay there now?'

'They paid me double commission.'

'Whatever for?'

'Getting you to buy that rotten champagne. Not many people fall for it.'

'You—you—' He was speechless.

'Please, Nick, be understanding. It's a good job.'

'What about loyalty?' he demanded furiously. 'You saw what they did to me.'

'You said they didn't hurt you.'

'It wasn't very dignified, though.'

'But you brought it on yourself by being heavy handed.'

'I was only trying to protect you,' he yelled.

'I didn't need protecting,' she yelled back.

'I might have known you wouldn't have changed,' he said through gritted teeth. 'The Poison Pixie still lives, doesn't she?'

'I've told you, don't call me that.'

'It's nothing to what I'd *like* to call you.'

'None of it would have happened if you hadn't started

throwing your weight around, talking to me as if I were an idiot who didn't know what she was doing…'

'Don't get me started on that subject,' he grated.

'I've got my life organised very nicely, and I don't need you telling me what to do.'

'I think that's exactly what you need.'

Katie drew herself up to her full height. This still left her looking up eight inches into his face, but she managed a kind of quelling dignity.

'I'm not going to discuss this any more, Nick. The subject is closed. Goodnight.'

She went to her room. Nick opened his mouth to protest, but for the second time that night he found himself staring at a closed door.

Nick meant to be graciously forbearing over breakfast. But Katie didn't show up, and it was hard to be forbearing to a grapefruit. He added it to the list of her sins.

But by evening he'd forgiven her, and even started to worry about her journey home so late at night. He had dinner with a client, and then, much against his better judgement, headed for the Pop-Eyed Parrot.

After half an hour Katie emerged from the rear entrance in a glum little side street, and headed for the night bus stop. She seemed more tired and less full of vitality than he'd ever seen her.

'Katie!' he called.

It was typical of her that she'd forgotten her annoyance of the night before. She smiled when she saw him, and ran the few steps to the car. 'My own private chauffeur! How luxurious!' she said, snuggling down in the passenger seat. 'Oooh, it's so lovely to sit down. My feet are killing me.'

'Waitressing can't be doing them any good,' he observed, easing the car gently into the traffic.

'Do you mind?' she said with mock severity. 'Waitress indeed! I'm a wine hostess!'

'That's just what your employer calls it to make you feel good, so that he can pay you slave labour rates.'

'Plus my extra commission,' she teased him provocatively.

'Let's not talk about that champagne and what I had to pay for it. Katie, for Pete's sake! Why must you—?' He stopped and ground his teeth. 'No need to ask. I know the answer. You're off your head!'

She sighed sleepily. 'You say such charming things.'

'My thoughts aren't at all charming. Of all the awkward, troublesome, bird-brained—' Words failed him.

She didn't answer back, which gave him the chance to organise his thoughts. 'It's time we had a serious talk, Katie, about where you're going. You must see that things can't continue this way. I won't always be here to take you home, and heaven knows what—'

The lights were changing as he approached. He slowed to a halt and turned to her.

Katie was asleep.

'You see what I mean?' he asked her sleeping form. 'You can't go on wearing yourself out, doing an unsuitable job that—'

Horns tooting irritably warned him that the lights had changed to green and he was holding up the traffic. Katie had made him forget the outside world. He drove on thoughtfully.

He parked the car in the underground car park of the apartment block, and nudged her gently. 'We're here.'

She got out in a slow, hazy sort of way that suggested

she was walking in her sleep. When Nick had locked up he found her leaning against the car with her eyes closed.

'Come on,' he said, giving her a little nudge.

She didn't awaken, so he took hold of her shoulders and shook her gently. But this only made her slide against him, her head on his shoulder.

'Katie, we're home.'

'Mmm?'

'Poor kid, you're worn out, aren't you?'

'Mmm,' she agreed.

'Come on. Let's get upstairs.'

He lifted her carefully and made his way to the lift. It was just possible to move the hand under her knees enough to press the button. To his relief, the lift was empty.

She weighed almost nothing, and it was easier to keep her in his arms for the short journey to the third floor. As the lift climbed, a strange thing happened to him. He no longer cared whether there would be anybody around to see them. All his attention was taken up by the sweetness of holding her, the soft tickle of her hair against his neck, the faint sound of her breathing. After a while he looked up to see that the doors were open. He didn't know how long they'd been that way.

There was nobody in the hall. From upstairs he could hear the sound of laughter and the chink of glasses, which meant there was another party going on.

The apartment was in darkness, except for the light coming through the windows that overlooked the river.

'Katie,' he said softly. But the only sound was the steady rhythm of her breathing.

'Katie,' he repeated. 'We're home. Time to wake up and go to bed.'

Her breath, whispering past his chin, gave him a sensation that he couldn't define. He stood, irresolute, with her in his arms. At last he nudged the door of her room open with his foot, and carried her inside.

As he laid her down on the bed she instinctively clasped her arms about his neck to steady herself. He leaned right down, so as to lower her smoothly. It might have been an accident that his lips brushed against hers. At any rate, he hadn't meant to do it, but the next moment it was done. He stood, tense with shock, waiting for her to awaken and berate him, but she didn't. She was deeply asleep—far too deeply to know what had happened, he assured himself.

He hastily released her. Her arms were still locked about his neck and he disengaged them as gently as possible, so not to awaken her. Moonlight coming through the window showed him her face, peaceful and vulnerable. Suddenly he wanted to kiss her properly, and for a wild instant he nearly yielded to temptation. He stood watching her, fighting himself, overwhelmed by both tenderness and desire. Then Katie rolled away and curled up in a position of contentment, and he was able to force himself back from the bed.

He found a blanket in the cupboard and draped it over her. Then he got out as fast as he could.

CHAPTER SIX

NICK wondered how he could face Katie next morning. Had she been conscious of that kiss? But the heartless creature was up before him, sitting at the breakfast bar, wolfing down toast and honey as if there was no tomorrow.

'How can you eat all that stuff and stay slim?' he asked, revolted.

'I get a lot of exercise,' she said cheerfully. 'I don't sit around at a desk all day, like some people.'

'If that's meant for me it's a slander.'

'True. You don't just sit around at a desk. Sometimes you get up and walk to your expensive car. Then you sit in that.'

'It might interest you to know,' he said stiffly, 'that my firm has a policy of encouraging its executives to stay fit, which is why there's a fully equipped gymnasium on the premises.'

'You sound like a promotional leaflet. Besides, when did you last use the gym?'

'That isn't the point.'

'Of course it is. It's no good just having it there. You have to visit it occasionally, and do things with weights and levers. Someone should have explained that to you. Perhaps you didn't read the right leaflets.'

'Will you be leaving soon?' he asked coldly.

'Yup. I'm on my way.' She slung the bag with her practice kit over her shoulder and departed, whistling.

Nick was left wondering how he could ever have seen her as anything but a thorn in his side.

Having begun badly, the day continued badly. He found himself sharing a lift down to the car park with Leonora, from the flat above. She looked bright-eyed, and not in the least like someone who'd enjoyed a late party.

'We didn't disturb you last night, did we?' she asked cheerfully.

'Not in the least.'

'Sorry if we did, and all that. Only we get carried away sometimes. It's lucky these places are sound-proofed. We got a bit merry to celebrate me starting work on the long hauls. I'm off to New York today.' She gave a horsy laugh.

'And when you get back, I expect you'll be celebrating again,' Nick observed.

'I say, what a good idea! Thanks a lot.'

They'd reached the car park by now. Leonora got into her car and drove jauntily away, leaving Nick to reflect that he had only himself to blame.

'Oh, dear!' Lilian said sympathetically when he told her. 'You're really having a terrible time with that girl, aren't you?'

'Oh, she's not so bad,' he said tolerantly.

They were having a quiet dinner together, and Nick was feeling better under the soothing effects of her Isobel-type good sense.

'It's like you to make the best of it,' Lilian said with an understanding smile, 'but I can see she's a bit of a strain.'

'Just a bit,' he admitted, remembering the strain he'd endured the previous night, stifling the impulse to kiss

Katie. He gave a reluctant laugh. 'The worst of it is, she says the most outrageous things and they stick. I actually went to the gym today.'

'But you're extremely fit.'

'I know, but Katie made me feel like Orca the whale, although she was just winding me up.'

'She should know better. As for making you collect her from that nightclub—'

'It was my idea. I don't like to think of her travelling home alone.' He looked at his watch. 'I'll have to be going for her soon.'

Lilian was silent. Only the drumming of her fingers betrayed her annoyance.

'When will Derek be back?' she asked at last.

'Not for a week or so. Why? Oh, you mean he could collect her?'

'No, there's something else—rather a delicate matter. Katie's very young. She's needs protecting.'

'That's what I'm doing.'

'But, darling, you're not. With Derek and Patsy gone, you and she are living alone together. Of course, everyone's more relaxed about that kind of thing these days, but even so, a young man and woman sharing an apartment—people are bound to think—' She stopped.

'That Katie and I—? Not a chance. She's the last person on earth that I'd want to—' He stopped, invaded by memories of carrying her in his arms, feeling her lips brush against his.

'Well, naturally. You're a man of taste, and she—well.' Lilian gave her silvery laugh.

He had a disagreeable sensation, as though she'd trodden on his toe. It flashed through his mind that Isobel would never have said anything with that ill-natured edge. And nor, come to think of it, would Katie.

Of course Katie often gave him a piece of her mind, and it was seldom flattering. But it was straight out to his face, and he'd never heard her say anything remotely unkind about anyone else.

'Darling, are you listening to me?' Lilian asked.

'Yes—er—sorry, what were you saying?'

'I was telling you about the YWCC—Young Women's Care and Concern. It's a charity I work with. They run hostels for people like Katie: only female residents, and no men allowed in the rooms. It's to stop innocent girls falling into the hands of undesirables.'

'Then it's no place for Katie,' he said with a grin. 'She seems to make a beeline for every undesirable in town.'

'That's why you should insist. She's vulnerable, Nick, and it's your duty to protect her.'

'You're right,' he admitted.

'The place I have in mind is called Hendon House. It's only two streets away from the Pop-Eyed Parrot, and they could take her straight away.'

'You fixed it before you spoke to me?' he asked, frowning.

'I checked that they had a vacancy. It would have been silly not to,' she said reasonably.

It was quite logical. He couldn't have said why he suddenly wanted to resist her. But she was more right than she knew, he reflected guiltily. For Katie's sake, he had to put a distance between them.

'I'll tell her tonight,' he agreed.

'I knew you'd see it my way,' Lilian purred. 'Well, I think it's time we were going.' She stood up and brushed her skirt down, then gave him a small puzzled frown. 'Nick, why are you looking at my ankles?'

'I'm not,' he said quickly. 'Let's go.'

*   *   *

As before, Katie was drooping with sleep, and said little on the journey home. When he swung around a corner she slid gently over until her head was resting against his shoulder. He knew he should push her away, but it would have meant taking a hand off the wheel, and he decided it would be safer not to. She was so light that he barely felt anything, yet he was aware of her every breath.

When the car stopped he shook her gently awake. 'Katie, it's time to wake up.'

'I don't want to,' she murmured sleepily. 'I was having such a lovely dream.'

'You can have it again when you're in bed.'

'No, I'll have lost it,' she sighed. 'Dreams never come back, do they, Nick?'

'I suppose not. You'll have to make do with another one.'

'You can't "make do" with dreams. It has to be the right one. It's no good pretending one person is another.'

'What was that?'

She looked at him directly. 'Lilian isn't Isobel, Nick.'

'Never mind that,' he said quickly. 'Come on, out of the car.'

It would be a relief to be rid of her. From now on there would be nobody sending him up and finding his weak spots. Not that Lilian was a weak spot, he amended hastily. She had her own virtues, which Katie couldn't possibly appreciate.

In the lift she leaned tiredly against the wall, but he resisted the temptation to put his arm around her. The neon light in the ceiling drained the colour from her face, emphasising the dark shadows under her eyes and a look of strain that he hadn't noticed before.

Then she opened her eyes and smiled mischievously. 'Do I look awful?' she asked.

'Awful,' he agreed gently. 'It's not doing you any good, these late nights and then the long journey.'

'You don't mind picking me up, do you?' she asked anxiously.

'I can't keep doing it, Katie. I had to leave Lilian early tonight just to come for you.'

'I see,' she said quietly. 'And she didn't like that?'

'She was charming about it. *I'm* the one who didn't like it. I don't mean that I dislike helping you, but Lilian and I—that is, I do have my own life to live.'

'With Lilian? Oh, Nick, you're not going to marry her, are you?'

'Katie, for heaven's sake!' he said, half-laughing, half-annoyed. 'Mind your own business, you little wretch!'

'But are you?'

'Probably! If I ever get the chance to court her,' he said, goaded.

When they were in the apartment he said, 'Katie, we have to talk.'

'No need. I'll get myself home in future.'

'Not all the way out here. If you must work in that place you need to live nearer. Lilian knows somewhere close by that you can stay. It's near your dance studio too.'

She whirled to face him, her face outraged. '*Lilian* knows a place? Have you been discussing me with her?'

'I discuss everything with Lilian.'

'And she's arranged where she wants me to live?'

'She saw I was worried and found a way to help me. Lilian takes an interest in all my problems.'

'So now I'm a problem?'

'Finding you somewhere to live was a problem. Try to understand, Katie. I never reckoned on having you here more than a couple of weeks, and you've already stayed longer than that. I've loved your visit, but—'

'No, you haven't. You've hated it. I've always gotten on your wrong side and been a pain in the neck. You said so.'

'That was ages ago. Surely we've become friends since then?' He looked at her coaxingly. 'Haven't we?' When she wouldn't answer Nick lifted her chin with his fingers. 'Aren't we friends?'

She shrugged. 'Anyone can be friends.'

'No, friendship is very difficult, but we managed it against all the odds. Remember when we used to hate each other like poison?'

'Yes,' she said with a shaky smile.

'And we don't any more, do we?'

'Nope.'

'You'll like this place.'

'You've seen it?'

'No, Lilian only mentioned it tonight.'

'Then you can't know if I'll like it or not.'

'I know Lilian would never suggest anywhere unsuitable. It's run by Young Women's Care and Concern. They're very respectable and—and caring...' he said uneasily.

She faced him, hands on hips. 'In other words, it's a prison?'

'Of course not. Stop twisting everything I say. You need protecting—'

'From what?'

'Well—you—me—alone here together—'

'You mean people will think you have designs on my

person? We can't be alone without you wanting to carry me off to bed and ravish me?'

'Katie, please—' he said, reddening.

'*Do* you have designs on my person, Nick?'

'Certainly not,' he said robustly, banishing certain awkward memories.

'Are you quite sure?'

With a start of horror he saw how he must look to her. At twenty-nine, he regarded himself as a young man in his prime, but to Katie he was past it. If she guessed how she'd affected him as she lay in his arms she would despise him.

'Katie,' he said firmly, 'you're the last woman on earth I'd want to ravish. I mean—not that I ever—if I did—not that I would—*hell!*'

'Oh, Nick,' she said with a sigh. 'Oh, Nick!' She turned away to the kitchen area and put the kettle on, banging things about in a stormy way.

'Katie, you've got to believe me. I've never thought of you in that way, not for a second. What's more,' he added, becoming inspired, 'I know I never could. I like a woman to be mature, a little experienced and sophisticated. Young innocents just don't attract me.'

'So my virtue is safe?'

'Safe as houses. The thought of making love to you has never once crossed my mind.'

'Well, thanks for telling me I look like the back of a bus!'

'No, you're very pretty,' he said, determined not to let her rile him, 'and I can understand why all the others are mad about you. But with us the past gets in the way. You've got used to seeing me as an elderly uncle, and I've got used to seeing you as the Poison Pixie. I guess that's it.'

'I notice you didn't mention Lilian. You might have said, "I can't fancy you, Katie, because I'm madly in love with Lilian." But you didn't.'

'Stop trying to wind me up.'

'But aren't you in love with her, Nick?'

'Yes,' he said firmly. 'I am.'

'And you really want me to go?' she asked in a small voice.

'It's best for both of us,' he said gently.

'All right, Nick. I'll do whatever you want.'

'It's for your sake, Katie,' he said awkwardly.

She patted his arm. 'Of course it is. Let's not say any more. When do you want me out?'

'Don't talk as though I was evicting you into the snow,' he begged. 'You can have a couple of days to get your things together, and then Lilian and I will drive you there.'

'Lilian's coming?'

'Well, it was her idea.'

'Yes, it was, wasn't it?' she said in a colourless voice.

Two days later Katie had an evening off. Lilian and Nick drove to his flat after work, to collect her, and found Katie packed and ready. Her face wore a stricken look that Nick had never seen before, and he was suddenly full of misgivings.

They increased when he saw the grim building where the YWCC was housed. With its rows of matched windows, it might once have been an office block—or even, as Katie had suspected, a prison.

The inside was even less welcoming. The large hallway was poorly lit. The walls were painted grey, adorned by glum pastel landscapes. On one wall hung a

list of rules that began, 'WELCOME TO HENDON
HOUSE...'

'Lilian,' Nick said uneasily, 'perhaps—'

'Can I help you?' A large middle-aged woman was
bearing down on them.

'This is Miss Katherine Deakins,' Lilian said graciously. 'I made a booking for her.'

'Certainly. I'm Mrs Ebworth. Welcome to Hendon
Hall.' She made it sound like a pronouncement of doom.

'Thank you,' Katie said uncertainly.

'We expect all our young ladies to be happy here.'
Her tone implied dire retribution for anyone who failed
to be happy. 'Here's your personal copy of the rules.'

She produced a sheet of paper with the air of one
conferring a blessing, and Katie accepted it meekly.

'We prefer our residents to read the rules at the start,
so that we can get everything straight,' Mrs Ebworth
declared. 'You will note that no male persons are allowed in your room at any time, night or day. Nor is
alcohol. The outer door closes sharp at midnight.'

'But I sometimes work until two in the morning,'
Katie protested.

Mrs Ebworth's face was beginning to set in lines of
rigidity when Lilian intervened. 'I'm sure an exception
can be made, since Katie's job depends on it,' she said
sweetly.

'In that case, very well,' Mrs Ebworth said coldly.

Nick was becoming more worried. He disliked Mrs
Ebworth, who was clearly worthiness personified, but
had none of Patsy's motherly warmth.

'Now I'll show you to your quarters,' Mrs Ebworth
said grandly.

As they went up in the lift Nick tried to reassure himself with visions of a cosy little haven. They vanished

when he saw the small, sparsely furnished room. It had a narrow bed, which looked hard, a wardrobe, dressing table and washbasin. On the walls were more of the same miserable pastels as downstairs. The floor was covered with a thin, functional carpet.

Against this dreary background Katie stood out like a rich ruby against lead. She looked around at her new 'home', and Nick saw the stunned look on her face. That decided him.

'I don't think this is a good idea,' he said.

'Nonsense, darling, this is very suitable,' Lilian insisted.

'There's great demand for our accommodation,' Mrs Ebworth said. 'I could have filled this room a dozen times over.'

'So it won't inconvenience you if Miss Deakins doesn't come here after all?' Nick asked quietly.

'Good heavens, Nick, you can't do that at the last moment,' Lilian exclaimed, with a brittle smile. 'I pulled strings to get Katie moved to the head of the queue.'

'Lilian, look at this place,' he said urgently.

'What's wrong with it? It's clean, and convenient for her work.'

'But it's hardly cosy, is it?'

Katie spoke for the first time. 'This is fine. In fact it's perfect in every way.'

'Katie,' he said urgently. 'What are you playing at?'

'I thought I was doing what you want.'

'I don't want this for you.'

Lilian laid a hand on his arm. 'Darling, if Katie is satisfied—and I must say I think she's very wise—then who are we to argue?'

'I'm extremely happy with it,' Katie announced defiantly.

He didn't believe a word, and he was hurt by the sight of her determinedly cheerful face. Then suddenly he drew a sharp breath. It was there again, the haunting likeness to Isobel that wouldn't leave him alone. If he could only define it, perhaps it would cease to trouble him.

'I'm taking you home,' he said firmly.

He heard Lilian's gasp of annoyance, and saw Katie's chin set in lines of stubbornness.

'This is my home now, Nick. And I'm staying. As Lilian says, it's central, and your flat isn't. I'll be much safer here.'

'I suppose so…' he said unwillingly.

'I'll soon make it look homely,' Katie added. 'I'm staying. It's all decided.'

'You see? I told you it was for the best,' Lilian said. 'Katie, dear, let me help you unpack.'

'Thank you, but I'll do it when you've gone. I expect you two want to get on with your date.'

'That's very sweet of you,' Lilian purred.

Nick laid a hand on Katie's arm. 'You'll call me if you need anything?' he said urgently.

'Of course I will. Goodbye.'

'Don't be in such a hurry to get rid of me. Here, I've got you a present.'

He gave her a package he'd been holding, and smiled as she unwrapped it. It was a compact digital radio, cassette and CD-player.

'Oh, Nick, that's lovely of you.' Katie threw her arms around his neck in gratitude. 'Thank you, thank you,' she whispered.

She came down to the front door with them, chattering eagerly, her face wreathed in smiles. Not until they'd driven away did she allow the smile to be replaced by a look of misery.

It was strange to Nick how empty the flat seemed when Katie had gone. She'd filled it with her presence; her maddening presence, he'd thought. But now he forgot the maddening part, and remembered her brightness and infectious gaiety.

He'd always been proud of his splendid apartment, and the way it underlined his success. Now he saw that it was only a residence, not a home. In fact, without Katie it was dead. She was untidy, she forgot things, lost them, then remembered them at awkward moments. She'd driven him distracted with her scatty ways, but she'd taken sunshine wherever she went.

Once he found a shoe of hers lying in the corner of the living room. He recalled how she'd kicked them off and wriggled her toes as soon as she got home. The dainty shoe looked forlorn without its mate. Almost as forlorn as himself.

Returning it would be a perfect excuse to visit her, but the realisation that he was seeking excuses gave him a sense of danger. He put the shoe in an envelope and mailed it.

It was just that he wasn't used to living alone, he decided. It would be better when Derek was there. He actually found himself looking forward to his erratic flat-mate's return.

He missed the exact moment when it happened, but one evening he arrived home to find a 'Quiet Please' sign on Derek's door. He made himself a light meal, and was eating it while reading the *Financial Times* when Derek appeared, bleary-eyed.

'What time is it?' he yawned.

'Nearly ten in the evening. When did you get in?'

'A couple of hours ago.'

'Did you have a successful trip?'

'Fantastic. I'll be a millionaire at this rate. Why is it so quiet? Where is everybody? Patsy, Katie...?'

'Patsy had to visit one of her sons, who was having domestic trouble, and Katie has found somewhere else to live.'

Derek stopped rubbing his eyes. 'You mean you threw her out?' he demanded.

'That's not what I said—'

'I know what you said, and I'll bet it wasn't Katie's idea to go.'

'Will you stop striding up and down? You're shaking the floor. Katie had to go, for her own sake. She and I couldn't live here alone.'

'I see Lilian's hand in this.'

'She was concerned for Katie's welfare—'

'I'll bet that's not all she was concerned about,' Derek said shrewdly. 'How could you do this to Katie?'

'She likes her new place,' Nick said firmly. 'She said so. Hey, where are you going?' Derek was striding back to his room.

'To rescue a damsel in distress,' he called over his shoulder.

Katie finished serving her last customer and breathed a sigh of relief. Her feet hurt, her head hurt, in fact everywhere hurt, including her heart. These days, it was harder to keep up her usual high spirits. She thought of Hendon House, where she would have to creep in, hoping that for once Mrs Ebworth wouldn't be peering over the banisters, lips pursed in disapproval. Life, which had seemed so brilliant a few weeks ago, had now taken on a grey and dreary air.

She changed hurriedly, and headed for the rear exit. As she stepped onto the pavement someone touched her arm. She whirled and found herself looking into two laughing eyes.

'Hallo, Katie,' Derek said.

She cried out eagerly, and enveloped him in a hug. He hugged her back with enthusiasm. 'We need somewhere to talk,' he said.

'I've got to get back to the prison camp soon, or there'll be trouble,' she said dramatically.

'Good grief! What have you got into?'

Luckily they managed to creep in unobserved. Derek looked around him, noting the bleakness of the room, and Katie's attempts to make it cheerful.

'This'll make you feel better,' he said, producing a bottle of champagne. 'Unless you get it free at work?'

'You're joking. My boss says champagne isn't for drinking, it's for turning into money.' She chuckled. 'As Nick found out.'

She filled her toothmug and sipped the sparkling liquid with an expression of bliss. Derek declined because he was driving.

'What was that about Nick?' he asked.

She told the story of Nick's ill-fated visit to the club, and Derek shouted with laughter. 'He paid *how much* for it?'

'Shh!' she said frantically. 'You'll awaken the prison warder.'

'Sorry, sorry.' He looked around him and spotted the new radio. 'That's nice.'

'Isn't it lovely?' Katie beamed. 'Nick gave it to me.'

'As a goodbye present?'

'Not goodbye,' she said quickly. 'We're still in the same city, and I'll be seeing him—some time.'

Derek took her hand. 'You'd better tell me everything,' he said kindly.

It was a relief to talk. Derek was a good listener, and the story stretched on through the night, while the level of the champagne went down.

'Something's got to be done about this,' Derek declared at last.

'Like what?'

'Don't worry, I'll think of a master plan. Now perhaps I'd better go. You're getting a bit tiddly.'

'Am I really?' She hiccuped, and giggled. 'I guess I am.' Suddenly everything seemed terribly funny.

He began to laugh with her. Although he hadn't touched the champagne, he was getting light-headed from lack of sleep.

'Finish it up,' he said, preparing to pour.

Katie held out her glass in the rough direction of the bottle, but somehow she missed, and the champagne went all over her. They both grabbed for the heavy bottle, but it slithered out of their fingers and bounced noisily on the floor. This struck them as hilarious, and they clung together in an ecstasy of mirth.

'Hush!' they told each other frantically.

But it was too late. There was a noise outside. The next moment the door was flung open, and Mrs Ebworth stood on the threshold, with a face of doom.

NO RISK, NO OBLIGATION TO BUY...NOW OR EVER!

GUARANTEED

PLAY "ROLL A DOUBLE" AND YOU GET FREE GIFTS! HERE'S HOW TO PLAY:

1. Peel off label from front cover. Place it in space provided at right. With a coin, carefully scratch off the silver dice. Then check the claim chart to see what we have for you – TWO FREE BOOKS and a mystery gift – ALL YOURS! ALL FREE!

2. Send back this card and you'll receive brand-new Harlequin Romance® novels. These books have a cover price of $3.50 each, but they are yours to keep absolutely free.

3. There's no catch. You're under no obligation to buy anything. We charge nothing – ZERO – for your first shipment. And you don't have to make any minimum number of purchases – not even one!

4. The fact is, thousands of readers enjoy receiving books by mail from the Harlequin Reader Service®. They like the convenience of home delivery...they like getting the best new novels BEFORE they're available in stores...and they love our discount prices!

5. We hope that after receiving your free books you'll want to remain a subscriber. But the choice is yours – to continue or cancel any time at all! So why not take us up on our invitation, with no risk of any kind. You'll be glad you did!

The Harlequin Reader Service®— Here's how it works:

If offer card is missing write to: Harlequin Reader Service, 3010 Walden Ave., P.O. Box 1867, Buffalo NY 14240-1867

BUSINESS REPLY MAIL
FIRST-CLASS MAIL   PERMIT NO. 717   BUFFALO, NY

POSTAGE WILL BE PAID BY ADDRESSEE

HARLEQUIN READER SERVICE
3010 WALDEN AVE
PO BOX 1867
BUFFALO NY 14240-9952

NO POSTAGE
NECESSARY
IF MAILED
IN THE
UNITED STATES

CHAPTER SEVEN

Two days later, Nick drove home in the afternoon, meaning to spend the rest of the day studying files. He inched his car in beside Leonora's showy vehicle, concentrating hard, so that he barely heard the murmur of female voices. But one of them sounded familiar...

'Katie!'

She ran to him, smiling. 'Hallo, Nick. You're not usually home so early.'

'Never mind me,' he said, getting out. 'What are you doing here?'

'I live just above you now. Leonora and her friends had a spare place in their flat, and they let me have it.'

He felt as though the breath had been knocked out of his body. This couldn't be happening.

'Come upstairs,' he said. 'We have to talk about this.'

'I can't. Leonora's driving me to work.'

'And who'll bring you home?'

'Derek. He fixed everything. Wasn't that kind of him?'

'Yes, wasn't it?' he echoed grimly. 'You can't stay up there. The kind of life they lead is—isn't— Please, Katie, be reasonable. Go back to Hendon House.'

'I'm afraid they wouldn't take me,' Katie said abjectly. 'I was ordered out for "lewd and disgusting behaviour".'

'You were *what*?'

'Entertaining men in my room at four in the morning,'

she said, with a sigh of contrition that didn't fool him
for a moment.'

'*Men?* Plural?'

'Well, no, there was only Derek, actually. But, as Mrs
Ebworth so rightly said, it was the principle that counted.
One bad apple like me could cause havoc among the
others. She was very kind, though. She let me stay until
seven in the morning, so that I could sleep off my
drunken orgy.'

'Your—?' Nick echoed glassily.

'She said there was strong drink everywhere,' Katie
finished.

Nick stared, beyond speech.

'Katie, we have to be going,' Leonora called.

'Coming! Bye, Nick. See you some time—maybe.'
She vanished with a cheery wave.

Derek was at home, stretched out on the sofa, gazing
into the middle distance.

'Just tell me one thing,' Nick said in a dangerous
voice, when he'd slammed the door. 'Were you in
Katie's room at four in the morning?'

'Yes, I was.' Something in Nick's eyes made Derek
leap smartly from the sofa and put a table between them.

'*Doing what?*'

'Listening to her.'

'Like hell!'

'Listening was what she needed. She had to get out
of that morgue.'

'Thanks to you,' Nick said through gritted teeth, 'she
was *thrown* out for being a bad influence on the others.

Derek gave a yelp of laughter. 'I know. We thought
that was hilarious.'

'You would. And what's this about a drunken orgy?'

'One bottle of champagne—but a really good vintage,' Derek added provocatively. 'Well worth the price.'

'I needn't ask what that means. I trust the two of you had a good laugh at my expense?'

'Fair to middling.'

'I might have known you couldn't be back five minutes without causing trouble. What were you thinking of to send her to Leonora?'

'Quit making a fuss! They're just a few lively girls.'

'They have wild parties that go on all night. The place is a hotbed of immorality.'

'It can't be. I know them all.'

'So I would have supposed,' Nick informed him coldly.

Derek was becoming perturbed. 'It isn't really a hotbed of immorality—is it?'

'I'm sure you have your own standards.' Nick ripped off his jacket and began to make himself strong coffee, muttering furiously. 'I wouldn't put anything past you. I should have known better than to introduce you to an innocent girl. Heaven knows what kind of damage...'

Derek had moved to the kitchen area and was following Nick about in agitation. 'Are you *sure* it's a hotbed of immorality?'

'Certain.'

'Well, I'll be—! Nobody ever told me about it.' Derek sounded injured. 'The most I've ever been offered up there is cooking sherry.'

'Well, you've really done it this time. I blame you for everything that happens to Katie from now on.'

He collected her from work himself that night, almost forcibly restraining Derek when he tried to assume the task. Katie saw him as soon as she left the club, and waved merrily.

'You don't seem entirely surprised to see me,' he observed as she tucked herself into the car beside him.

'I knew you'd want to have your say. And if you're going to slag off Leonora you won't want her there.'

'I'm not going to 'slag off' anybody, merely point out the danger you're running.'

'Nick, I honestly couldn't have stayed in Hendon House.'

'You could if you hadn't engaged in a drunken debauch with the Romeo of the software world,' he said stiffly.

She burst out into a laugh that would have annoyed him if he hadn't been listening to its rich, generous quality.

'Oh, Nick,' she gasped, holding her stomach, 'if you could only hear yourself. You sound like Mrs Ebworth.'

'No need to insult me,' he said, grinning reluctantly. 'I didn't like that place, but you said it was fine, or I'd have had you out of there the first day. Why did you pretend it was all right?'

She gave a quick sideways glance at his profile as he concentrated on the road. Perhaps she was searching for something that she didn't find, for she shrugged and said with a forced lightness, 'I was just being awkward, of course. You know me.'

'All right, it's done now, but you can't stay with all those hard-living young women. Isobel would have a fit. And she'll blame me,' he added after a moment.

'Well, if that doesn't beat all!' Katie exclaimed indignantly. 'You pretend to be worried for my safety, but you're only thinking of how you'll rate with Isobel.

Actually, Isobel's thrilled that I escaped from the prison where you dumped me.'

'You told her——?' he began, aghast.

'You just abandoned me, Nick,' Katie said with a little sniff. 'Isobel didn't like that.'

'I'll bet you laid it on with a trowel,' he seethed.

'Let's just say I enjoyed myself.'

'I refuse to rise to the bait, Katie. We have important things to discuss.'

'That won't take long. You say, "Katie, I order you out of the flat upstairs." I say, "Take a running jump." End of conversation.'

'Just listen. I know you're only up there because you can't afford a decent place on your own. So I'll help you out financially.'

Katie gave a dramatic gasp of horror. 'I can't take money from you, Nick. It wouldn't be proper, especially after all those things you said about my reputation. Why, I just don't know how you can even suggest such a thing to a respectable female——'

'All right, all right,' he said hastily.

'My flatmates are great. What have you got against them?'

'Didn't one of them spend a night in a police cell last week?'

'No, that was her boyfriend. She went to the station to bail him out.'

'And the wild parties?'

'Do they really have wild parties? What fun!'

He gave up. He knew Katie in this mood, presenting a mischievous surface that he couldn't get past. The suspicion that she was laughing at him made it worse.

At her front door he bid her a cool goodnight and returned to his own flat, mulling over the problem. The best thing to do was write to her, he decided. He would manage better when he could put his thoughts down calmly, with no Katie to get him agitated.

He took a lot of trouble over the letter, setting out his reasons coolly and rationally. He repeated his offer of money, and enclosed a cheque to emphasise that he meant business. He slipped the envelope under her door, and went downstairs with a feeling of relief. He was pleased by his own irresistible logic. She simply couldn't argue her way around it.

But next morning an envelope lay on his doormat. Inside was his cheque, and a note in large, defiant letters. It said simply: *'The Poison Pixie strikes again! Ha-ha!!!'*

After that there was peace for a while. He and Katie didn't trouble each other, or even speak beyond a polite hallo if they chanced to meet in the building. She always smiled and waved, but he thought her face was thinner, and dark circles were appearing under her eyes.

He discussed the problem with Lilian, but her mind was elsewhere. 'Darling, this was Katie's decision. We both did our best for her. She's made her own bed, and now she must lie on it.'

'I should have protected her better,' he groaned.

'We both tried, but she evidently doesn't want our protection. She's grown up. Now, let's talk about Mr Frayne and his exciting invitation.'

Eric Frayne was the Chairman of Devenham & Wentworth, Nick's bank, and he'd recently invited Nick and Lilian to dine at his house. They both knew what this meant. A job was about to become vacant, and Nick was eyeing it hopefully. His last promotion had been only a year ago, but he knew Mr Frayne thought well of him. Lilian was being looked over as an executive wife, a test that naturally she would pass with flying colours.

She talked eagerly about the evening to come. Nick tried to respond, but a cold hand was beginning to grip him. After this dinner party the job was probably his, and his marriage to Lilian would be drawing remorselessly closer.

On the big night Lilian was elegantly dressed in a dark blue classic gown. He had to admit she looked the role to perfection. They were the only guests at Eric's luxurious mansion, and he and his wife treated them like royalty. Lilian sat next to her host, laughing at his jokes, looking gracious, and never putting a foot wrong.

Nick could tell that Eric was impressed with both of them. Nobody mentioned the vacancy, but nobody thought of anything else. As he drove away he reflected that within a few weeks he could have the job he longed for and a wife who would be an asset to him. His heart was heavy.

Next morning he waited to be summoned to Eric's office, but the Chairman had gone out of town unexpectedly. He was away a week, and when he returned he didn't contact Nick. But he did invite another couple to dinner.

From almost relief Nick passed to dismay. The job was slipping away before his eyes, and he didn't know why. He couldn't discuss it with Lilian, who was showing a cool surprise at the delay which made him feel that he'd failed her. He found himself thinking of Katie, who would have teased him out of his glum mood. But it was over a week since their last encounter, and these days their relations were too distant for him to approach her.

One morning he was snatching a quick breakfast when

the phone rang. He answered with one eye on his watch.
'Yes?'

'I want to speak to Katie,' came an Australian voice
he recognised.

'Now, look, Ratchett, this has gone far enough. Katie
doesn't want to talk to you.'

'That's for Katie to say.'

'She *has* said.'

'I haven't come this far just to be fobbed off. I know
she'll see me when I've talked to her.'

'No way.'

'Fetch her, please.'

Nick slammed down the phone. In his mind he could
see Ratchett, a selfish, hard bitten man, pursuing his prey
from the other side of the world, determined to have his
own way no matter whom he hurt.

All the way to work Nick brooded on the problem.
He found a folder lying on his desk and stared at it,
wondering why it was familiar.

'It's your notes for your meeting with Mr Frayne,'
Patsy informed him.

'My what?'

'You're meeting him in an hour to discuss the Hallam-
Waines merger, and these last-minute conditions that
Holland's thrown up. Mr Frayne wanted your ideas
about dealing with him. All your notes are in here. You
know how important this could be,' Patsy added significantly.

Of course, he thought. Eric Frayne was waiting to see
how he handled this merger. If he made a success of it,
the job was his.

And it all had gone out of his mind because he was
worried about Katie. In the whole of his carefully
planned career he'd never made such a slip-up before.

Resolutely he pushed Katie to the back of his mind, and opened the folder. By the time he went into Eric Frayne's office he was alert again.

For an hour they worked steadily through other matters, then Mr Frayne mentioned the vacancy. 'I thought we'd have it settled by now. After John had that dizzy spell he wanted early retirement, and I started looking for his replacement. Now he's feeling better he's dragging his feet. I'll have a talk with him, persuade him that it's time to move on...'

Katie had moved on, but Ratchett didn't know, which was a blessing. One hint of that and his spies would ferret out her new address. He might even turn up on her doorstep...

'Er—sir?'

'I was saying the job needs varied talents, reliability, a gift for surprise, a hint of aggression.'

Ratchett had aggression. In fact it was odd that he hadn't already come calling. He was boxing clever, but soon his patience would run out. He would arrive and take Katie by surprise...

'A hell of a surprise,' he murmured.

'I admit surprise isn't everything,' Mr Frayne said, 'but it's something I value. Reliability is vital, but a man needs flair as well. Now, let's see your ideas about this merger.'

As they went through them Nick felt a stir of hope. He knew that reliability was his strong suit, and Mr Frayne made a number of approving comments.

'You've thought this through well,' he said, nodding. 'What do you think of the fuss Hallam's making over this three-way option?'

'He's in a strong position because Waines doesn't have much time to think,' Nick mused. 'He'd like to hold out, but he can't without our support. Would we be wise to give it? I'm not sure. I'd rather try to persuade him to compromise a little. Can I think this over a bit more?'

There was a silence. Eric Frayne was regarding him steadily, and with something in his eyes that Nick couldn't read.

'Let me have your final answer tomorrow morning,' he said at last. 'By the way, here's the analysis of Hallam's firm that you gave me the other day. Very thorough, very sound. Just what I'd have expected of you.'

Despite the praise, Nick had an uneasy feeling that he'd put a foot wrong. When he went over the conversation he was unable to work out where he'd erred, and that worried him more than anything. Then Katie's image rose again, and drove everything else out of his head.

He was swept by such a powerful desire to protect her that he forgot they were at odds. Tonight, he decided, he would catch her as she was going to work and make sure she was warned.

He worked late that evening, and went straight from his office to The Pop-Eyed Parrot, lingering by the rear entrance until the wine hostesses began to arrive. Nick watched closely, puzzled at not seeing Katie.

One of the young women spoke to him. 'You came to see Katie once, didn't you? I'm afraid she doesn't work here any more. She sprained her ankle last week and the manager chucked her out.'

As he drove back to the flat, he bitterly castigated Katie. How dare you not tell me? he demanded of her in his head. Of all the crazy, idiotic…

But when she answered her door, looking pale and strained, all he could find to say was, 'Poor Katie! You've really been in the wars, haven't you?'

'Kind of,' she said, with an attempt at a smile.

She was alone in the flat, and she took him into the kitchen for coffee.

'How did it happen?' he asked gently.

'I turned my ankle on those wretched heels. The manager said a limping parrot was no good to him. And then Mac…' Her voice wobbled slightly. 'Mac had found us an engagement, but I couldn't do it, so he got another partner. And he says he dances better with her than me. So that's that.'

She looked so woebegone that he instantly put his arms about her and hugged her tightly. She clung to him. 'Oh, Nick, why do I make a mess of everything?'

'You don't. It's their loss if they can't appreciate you.'

'I worked so hard; I really did. And then Mac just dumped me. And they're *my* routines they're doing. I worked out every step, but Mac just said, "Prove it," and I can't prove it, and everything's all gone wrong.'

'But why didn't you come to me?'

'Oh, you'd have been mad at me. You always said I'd come to no good.'

'I never did!.'

'I'll bet you've thought it often enough.'

'Never mind,' he said hastily. 'I'm not as bad as that! Am I?' He put his fingers under her chin and forced her to look up at him. 'Am I?' he repeated.

'No,' she admitted.

'Do you really think I'd crow because you're unhappy?'

She shook her head. 'I was just being hateful.'

'You're not hateful,' he said gently. 'You're depressed. How's your ankle now?'

'Fine. It's a week since I twisted it. I can dance again, but nobody wants me to.'

'Come and dance with me,' he said impulsively. The moment the words were out he was astonished. He hadn't meant to say them, but he seemed to be acting impulsively these days.

'Do you really mean it?' she asked eagerly.

'Sure I do. Where do you want to go?'

'Zoe's Place. It's a new club, nice and cheerful. You'll like it, Nick, really you will.'

Only when he was back in his room, changing, did he recall that he was supposed to be spending the evening mulling over the Hallam-Waines merger. He groaned, but it would be unthinkable to back out and disappoint Katie.

He knew he'd made the right decision when he saw her looking ravishing in an ankle-length white dress that shimmered as she moved. Even her hair shimmered from something she'd dusted onto it, and the sight of her enchanted Nick, driving everything else from his mind.

Zoe's Place was a nightclub with a small band. It was lively and cheerful, and Katie's dancing feet began skipping eagerly as soon as she was there.

'Come on,' she said, drawing him onto the floor. The dance was subtle and complicated, and at first he had qualms, but it was easy to follow her lead, especially when she smiled encouragement. Gradually Nick's confidence grew, his movements became rhythmic and he began to relax.

People were looking at them, admiring Katie, envying him his luck in being with her. He was escorting the most beautiful, talented woman in the place, and he loved it. As the music finished they clung together, laughing into each other's eyes as though they shared a secret.

'After that, I need a drink,' he said, laughing.

'Champagne?' she teased.

'Yes, champagne,' he said recklessly, and ordered the best vintage.

They toasted each other merrily. Nick was still caught up in the delight of dancing with Katie. At this moment he could have taken any risk, committed any recklessness. He felt better than ever in his life before.

Then he saw Eric Frayne.

His boss was sitting at a table with his wife, and they were both looking at Nick.

'I must just go and powder my nose,' Katie said, and tripped away.

Thoughts rushed pell mell through Nick's head. Katie— Lilian—the work he was supposed to be doing tonight—

But his next thought was, To hell with them all! He was having a wonderful time, and he didn't regret a thing.

Eric Frayne came over and greeted him genially. 'Our youngest is eighteen today and she's always wanted to come to Zoe's,' he said. 'So Mary and I decided to have her birthday celebration here. Never expected to see you in a place like this, though, especially with such a gorgeous young lady. You've got hidden depths, Nick.'

'She's my brother's sister-in-law,' Nick explained. 'I'm keeping an eye on her while she's in London.'

'So that's Katie,' Mr Frayne said, with a sudden movement of interest. 'Lilian mentioned her to me. I don't think she likes her. In fact, she seemed to think you might be in a bit of danger.'

'Lilian had no right to say any such thing,' Nick said furiously. 'Katie is none of her business.'

'Or mine?' Mr Frayne asked, with a faint smile.

'Don't answer that. It was on the tip of your tongue, that's all. And you're quite right.'

Katie appeared, and Nick made the introductions. Eric Frayne insisted that they join his table, and they went over to greet the rest of his family. His daughter was on the dance floor, but their nineteen-year-old son ogled Katie in astonishment. He was a displeasing youth, with a loose mouth.

'What a corker!' he muttered, while Katie was talking with Mrs Frayne. He would have said more, but the ferocious look in Nick's eyes made him fall silent. Eric Frayne watched and said nothing. After a while he asked Katie to dance with him, and the two of them took the floor, to the gleeful amusement of Eric's wife. He came back beaming with enjoyment.

'Haven't felt such a devil in years,' he confided to Nick. 'Clever young lady. Knows how to make a man feel good about himself. A real asset, that.'

When it was time to leave Eric said jovially, 'Hope you're not too tired to give the merger problem a think-through, Nick.'

What Nick said next took him by surprise even more than his listener. The words seemed to go straight from his instincts to his lips, bypassing his conscious brain.

'There's no need to think any more,' he said firmly. 'We should tell Waines to stand up to Hallam, and then we must support him up to the hilt.'

'You've changed your tune.'

'Hallam's a bully, and it's in our own interests to stop him, even if it means going out on a limb.'

'Fine. You go out on that limb first thing tomorrow morning. I leave it all to you.'

The two parties prepared to leave. Goodbyes were said. Mr Frayne shook Nick's hand. 'We learn something new about people every day, don't we?' he said enigmatically. 'See me as soon as you've dealt with Hallam.'

In the car, Katie sighed blissfully. 'That was a gorgeous evening,' she said.

'Yes, wasn't it?'

'Who is that man? I don't mean his name, but who *is* he?'

'He's my boss.'

'Oh, Nick!' Her hands flew to her mouth in horror. 'I called him a cheeky devil!'

'So I guessed. And don't worry. He loved it.'

He was on the phone to Hallam first thing next day. He'd come down from his high of the night before, but he was still feeling good. He knew now what the problem had been. His new-found confidence sustained him through a conversation that left Hallam feeling shellshocked.

The next call was to Waines, and was satisfactory on both sides. Nick made some hurried notes before going to see Mr Frayne, and found the Chairman just setting down his phone.

'That was Waines,' he said, beaming. 'Praising this firm to the skies for its willingness to take a stand. ''Vision'' and ''flair'' were among the words used. Well done, Nick. Excuse me a moment.'

He broke off to answer the phone. 'Mr Hallam—yes, I understand you've been talking to Mr Kenton—on the contrary, I knew his position in advance and fully support it—of course you usually deal with John Neen, but he's leaving, and since Mr Kenton will be taking over his job—I'm sure when you reconsider you'll see that he was right—I'll look forward to hearing from you.'

He hung up and regarded Nick, who was looking stunned.

'You managed to do the one thing I thought you'd never do,' Mr Frayne said. 'You surprised me. That was all I was waiting for. Congratulations. The job's yours.'

CHAPTER EIGHT

NICK celebrated his promotion with a new car. It was a sleek grey beauty, with pale leather upholstery, plenty of leg room and an engine that made almost no sound.

As was proper, he took Lilian for dinner and dancing, and she graciously admired his car and his promotion. He knew this was the right time to propose marriage, but something held him back. At a moment when life seemed to be carrying him towards her his heart was going in another direction.

Lilian was too much the lady to show annoyance. She uttered words of praise for his brains and subtlety. He smiled and thanked her. And it was all horribly wrong, because he really owed everything to Katie.

It wasn't just that she'd charmed his boss. Eric Frayne would never give him a job for such a reason. But she'd inspired Nick to break free and trust his instincts. His flair had always been there, deep down, smothered by caution. She'd liberated that flair, shown him a new side of himself. It was a side he liked, and not merely because it had brought him a better job.

He enjoyed taking Katie for a spin. Her admiration of the car was less gracious than Lilian's, but more whole-hearted, and she cheekily dubbed it the Silent Monster.

Their relationship had settled down to an amiable truce. Katie had found another job, working in a travel agency. 'Even you'll have to approve,' she teased.

'I'm not sure it would be wise for me to approve,' he

said, grinning. 'You might change jobs just to annoy me.'

'So I would.'

'Are they paying you enough to live on?'

'I'm fine, thank you,' she said, with a stubborn look that told him she wouldn't accept a penny from him. So life went on peacefully this way, until one day Katie was fired.

'How could I help it?' she asked Nick. 'That poor old couple had saved up for years for their second honeymoon, and what they were buying was a glossy, overpriced con trick. We've had loads of complaints about it. Of *course* I had to warn them. You must see that, Nick.'

'I do, but I'll bet your boss didn't.'

'He called me a traitor,' Katie said tragically. 'Then he fired me.'

'Well, if you can't manage the rent,' he found himself saying, 'you can come back to my place for a spell.'

To his astonishment she whirled on him, with a stormy face. *'I'd rather die,'* she flashed, and rushed out of the room.

She apologised later, and they made up, but he was left baffled. Katie's moods seemed to become more unpredictable by the day. Sometimes she was perfectly cheerful, but at others she seemed to keep him at arm's length.

There were three weeks to go before John Neen retired and Nick took over his job. He and Patsy were working hard to clear his desk and tie up all the ends.

'Nick,' Patsy said one morning, 'you're miles away.'

'Sorry,' he said hastily. 'I'm just worried about Katie and this Ratchett character.'

'Has he telephoned again?'

'No, but he's sent her a present. It arrived at my flat this morning, so I took it up to her. It was a diamond pendant.'

'A real diamond?'

'Real, perfect, and very expensive. The card said he thought of her every moment.'

'How nice!'

'Maybe. Or perhaps it was a threat, meaning she could never escape him.'

'You could take her away somewhere. In fact, you ought to have a vacation now, because once you've started John's job you won't be able to go.'

'That's a thought,' he mused. 'But where?'

'Why not borrow my little cottage?'

'I didn't know you had one.'

'It's on the Norfolk coast. There's Mainhurst, a nice little olde worlde village, with plenty of shops. You'll find Bay Cottage in good condition, because someone goes in to clean it and a handyman does the garden. She'll be safe from Ratchett and you can talk to her about how best to deal with him. Because this situation can't be allowed to go on.'

'Patsy, it's a great idea. But would she come away with me?' he wondered.

'Try her,' Patsy suggested with a twinkle.

Katie was still out of a job, and Nick found her looking pale and depressed. He wondered if it was his imagination that her light seemed dimmer these days, her cheerfulness a little forced. She didn't turn his suggestion down, but neither did she jump at it.

'Shouldn't you be taking Lilian?' she asked.

'Why do you say that?'

'Well, you and she—I mean, now you've got your

promotion—I thought you'd be saying something any day.'

'This has nothing to do with Lilian,' he said, after an uneasy pause. 'I don't think a seaside cottage would suit her. You've been looking peaky lately, and the sea air might put the roses back in your cheeks.'

'Are you sure you really want to take me?' she persisted.

'Katie,' he said gently, turning her face towards him. 'This isn't like you.'

'As long as I'm not a nuisance.'

He nearly said, That's never worried you before, in their old teasing way, but suddenly he couldn't. She was unhappy about something, and that hurt him.

'What's troubling you, Katie?' he asked gently. 'Tell Uncle Nick.'

'Nothing,' she said with a slight laugh. 'I'm just depressed about not having a job. I'd love to come to the cottage with you.'

'Great. We'll go on Friday.'

Nick spent Friday morning at work, leaving at noon to collect Katie from home. They set off for the country at one o'clock, but returned after ten minutes because she'd forgotten one of her bags. At one-thirty they set off again.

'I hope you've got everything this time,' Nick observed, 'because I'm not going back.'

'To hear you talk, anyone would think I was always forgetting things,' Katie said, sounding aggrieved.

He preserved a diplomatic silence.

As they neared the coast the heavens darkened and rain began to pelt down. The downpour lasted an hour, then stopped abruptly, and the sun came out, flooding the countryside with soft light. Soon they had their first glimpse of the sea. Katie whooped at the sight, and made him stop the car.

'I love the sea,' she cried, jumping out. 'When I was in Australia I learned to surf.'

'I don't think our waves are quite big enough for that,' he said, coming to stand beside her. 'But Patsy says the bathing's good, and there's a riding stable nearby.'

She hopped back into the car. 'Come on. Why are we wasting time?'

'Because you—' he began, and stopped with a grin. 'Let's get going.' It delighted him to see that she was bubbling and happy again.

Soon they were in the village of Mainhurst, which, as Patsy had promised, was full of picturesque charm. It was tiny, with a butcher, a baker, a chemist and a general store that doubled as a post office. They stopped to buy food and ask directions, and were told Bay Cottage lay 'just up ahead a bit'.

Soon they'd left the village behind. The road stretched ahead, with no sign of a cottage. Nick hailed a horseman, who said, 'Keep going along this road, toward Hallstone Bay, and you'll see the cottage.'

At last it came into sight, one lone building, facing the sea. The bay lay before it, the golden sand drenched in sun. Katie gave a gasp of delight, but Nick knew a stab of dismay at the isolation.

He'd pictured the cottage as part of the village. Nothing had warned him that he and Katie would be completely alone together, without another building for miles.

The cottage itself was enchanting, straight out of a picture book. It had a thatched roof and leaded windows. Roses and hollyhocks grew around the door, and doves cooed under the eaves.

Katie gave a delighted glance at the red flagstones, the open fireplace, the copper pots hanging from the ceiling. Then she bounded upstairs while Nick fetched the luggage.

A narrow wooden stairway led to the upper floor, where there was a tiny landing, a small, neat bathroom, and two bedrooms, both looking out over the bay.

'It's like a dream,' Katie said, rushing about excitedly. 'I never thought anywhere could be so beautiful.'

'You take this one,' Nick said, indicating the larger bedroom.

Katie dashed to the window. 'Just look at the sea!'

The sand stretched away, flat and empty, gleaming golden under the late afternoon sun. The two arms of the bay enclosed it, holding it apart from the world, perfect, inviting.

'Look!' She clutched his arm in excitement, pointing to the horizon. 'There's a rainbow.'

The multicoloured arch swung high into the heavens and plunged right down into the sea.

'Let's go swimming, Nick. Right now, while the rainbow's still there.'

'Shouldn't we unpack first?'

'The unpacking will wait and the rainbow won't,' she said, unarguably.

He grinned. 'All right.'

He hurriedly changed into swimming trunks, and ran downstairs to find Katie waiting by the front door. She wore a filmy flowered jacket that came halfway down her thighs. Beneath it Nick thought he could make out a dark bikini, but she bounded into action so fast that he couldn't be sure.

Katie grabbed his hand and dashed away to the beach. He followed her willingly, feeling all care fall away from him as he breathed in the salty air and felt the wind rush past him. Her hand was tiny in his, yet there was strength in the slim fingers, and he had a strange sensation, as though she were leading him not merely down a beach but out of darkness into sunlight. Actually, the sun was all around them, but the feeling of being led to a bright place persisted.

'The tide's coming in,' he said. 'Let's not get cut off.'

'The tide never comes right up the bay,' Katie said. 'It stops about ten yards away.'

'How on earth do you—?'

'Hurry, Nick,' she said with sudden urgency, as though she could hear the ticking of a clock that was inaudible to him. 'Let's leave our things here.'

They dropped the towels on the sand. Katie stripped off her filmy jacket, revealing a tiny black bikini. Her delicate figure was perfect, he thought in admiration. In her eagerness she took both his hands and danced backwards across the sand. Her smile enchanted him, and he couldn't help smiling back. Something had made Katie happy again, and her joy in life was irresistible.

Then she stumbled as her foot struck a half-submerged stone. He grasped her tightly to stop her falling, and for a devastating moment he could feel the soft skin of her body against his own. He released her, breathing hard, hoping she hadn't noticed how much she affected him.

Then she was free, running ahead, her long hair streaming out in the wind, leading him towards the rainbow.

Young Jane, Patsy's office junior, was new at her job. She'd put through Lilian's calls to Nick, but never seen her in the flesh. So when Lilian swept in, elegantly dressed in a charcoal power suit, with tiny diamond studs in her ears and wafting luxurious perfume, Jane was overwhelmed.

'Tell Mr Kenton that Miss Blake is here,' Lilian commanded.

'I'm afraid Mr Kenton has already left,' Jane said.

Lilian smiled graciously. 'You're new here, aren't you? But there's no need to give me the polite "line". I know that Mr Kenton is always at his desk on a Friday afternoon.'

'But he really isn't here, Miss Blake. He left early to spend a few days at Mrs Cornell's cottage.'

Lilian's smile faded. 'Then I'll see Mrs Cornell.'

'Come in, Miss Blake,' Patsy said from the doorway.

Lilian closed Patsy's door firmly behind her before saying, 'I didn't know you had a cottage, Patsy.'

'Just a little shack in the country,' Patsy said airily.

'Fine, well, if you'll just give me the address—'

'I'm afraid I couldn't do that.'

'Nonsense. Of course you can.'

'Nick didn't leave me any instructions about telling anyone,' Patsy said with perfect truth.

'This is absurd. I take it that you do know who I am?'

'Oh, yes, I know that.'

'And that Nick and I are practically—'

'Practically,' Patsy said. 'But not quite.'

Lilian's lips tightened. 'I see. I needn't ask whether that wretched girl has wheedled him into taking her with him. You do realise how much damage she can do him?'

'Nick's a big boy. He can take care of himself.'

'I'm not going to argue with you. I want to know where he is.'

'And I can't tell you without his specific instructions.'

'Very well. Call him now, and tell him I wish to speak

to him. I take it you're not rash enough to refuse to do that?'

'I'll be only too happy to call him for you, Miss Blake.' Patsy buzzed Jane on the intercom. 'Fetch my telephone book, please.'

'But I haven't got it, Mrs Cornell.'

'Oh, dear, I must have left it at home. Thank you, Jane.' She smiled blandly at Lilian. 'I'm afraid the number's gone right out of my head.'

Lilian breathed hard. 'I suppose you're content to let that stupid girl ruin him?'

'Katie isn't ruining him,' Patsy said. 'She's saving him. And I can promise you, she's far from stupid.'

'So am I,' Lilian said furiously. 'I warn you that when Mr Kenton returns I shall complain to him in the strongest possible terms.'

'In that case,' Patsy said, 'you'll need a complaint form. I've got some here—'

The door banged behind Lilian. After a moment Jane came in. 'She looks a real tartar,' she observed, awed.

'She's used to getting what she wants,' Patsy said.

'I wonder why she didn't just call his mobile.'

'She probably did, and found it switched off.'

'But Mr Kenton never turns it off.'

'*I* did that before he left. So either he hasn't found out, or he has found out and has left it off.' Patsy smiled reflectively. 'I wonder which.'

'That was good,' Nick said, wiping the remains of steak and peppers from his plate with a piece of bread. 'I didn't know you could cook.'

'I've got a dozen talents you don't know about,' Katie said, whisking his plate away. 'Ready for next?'

'I'm full,' he protested, patting his stomach.

'You won't even feel this, it's so light,' she promised.

She was right. The chilled syllabub weighed nothing and slipped down deliciously. Katie had taken charge of the cooking as soon as they'd arrived back from the beach. It was early evening, and as the sun had faded a nip had crept into the air, so she'd quickly started a log fire.

The great fireplace was made of brick, with a hearth big enough for sitting in. On one side was a bucket, full of wood, and on the other a rack hung with tongs and a poker. By the time the meal was over the fire was crackling merrily away. She tossed some very large cushions into the hearth and said, 'We'll have coffee by the fire.'

Nick settled himself in the depths of one of the cushions. The unaccustomed sea air and the energetic swim had made his body feel somnolent. It was blissful to lie back against the plump cushion, listening to the soft clinking noises she made in the kitchen. The scent of freshly perked coffee reached him, and he sighed appreciatively.

At last she came in with the coffee, plus a brandy glass with his favourite brandy, and plumped herself down on a fat cushion opposite him. She'd changed into a flowing caftan of autumn colours, and her sudden movement down jerked a gust of air up inside the neck, raising her hair so that it became fluffy in the firelight, like a halo.

'I never thought of you as domesticated,' he observed. 'At home you were never to be seen in the kitchen.'

'I boiled you an egg that time.'

'And burnt the egg saucepan,' he reminded her.

'Only because I thought the heat was off when it wasn't. I just didn't understand your dotty kitchen.'

'That was the very latest state-of-the-art ceramic hob,'

he protested. 'It never feels hot, so you don't burn yourself.'

'Well, what do I know about state-of-the-art hobs? We didn't have them in the bush.'

'In the bush?' he echoed, startled.

'There was just you and nature, fighting hand to hand,' she said dramatically. 'You trapped what you needed and roasted it slowly over a wood fire.'

'And what did you trap?' he asked, lips twitching.

'Whatever there was. If you haven't eaten a really juicy alligator, you haven't lived.'

He eyed her askance. 'Many alligators in Sydney, are there?'

She burst out laughing, and he laughed with her. 'Katie, you outrageous little fantasist!'

'But some of it's true. Dad and I did go into the bush once.'

'And got lost?'

'Well, no. We had an aboriginal guide who knew everywhere.'

'And *he* roasted the alligator?'

'No, he took us to a shop where they sold it in packs,' she admitted.

He choked into his brandy. Then he remembered something.

'Hey, I was going to ask you. How did you know about the tides here?'

'Patsy told me ages ago, when I first arrived and we went shopping together. We had a natter over lunch. The cottage has been in her husband's family for generations. When he died he left it to her. She comes here sometimes to think about him, and remember the lovely times they had.'

Nick was startled. 'She told you all that when you'd only just met?'

'We got on terribly well. Besides, I talked too. I told her all sorts of things about me.' Her eyes gleamed mischievously in the firelight. 'Things you've never dreamed of.'

He felt disconcerted. Patsy was a good friend, yet she'd told him little about her private life. But she'd opened up to Katie. Of course, women discussed personal things more easily than men. That was the explanation.

But not the only one. Warmth streamed from Katie, making her easy to talk to. Whereas he…

He shut that thought off hastily.

Nick regarded himself as a 'New Man'. But when he awoke to the smell of frying bacon, and went downstairs to find Katie making his breakfast, he had to admit to himself that he was in heaven.

'You shouldn't be doing all this,' he said as he sat down to a larger meal than he usually ate.

'Don't worry,' she said impishly. 'It's your turn tomorrow.'

'That's all right, then.'

Afterwards, she washed while he dried. Then they headed for the riding stables. He wasn't sure how good a rider she might be, but he was only slightly surprised when she picked the most spirited horse she could find. He chose an animal that was powerful but steady, and they set off together.

At first he was nervous for her, but she handled her fiery steed with confidence and authority. They galloped across country until they came to the shore, where they pulled up for a rest.

'It's so beautiful,' Katie said, looking along the miles of golden sand. 'I can't believe that we have it to ourselves. Why doesn't a beach like this attract holiday-makers?'

'Probably because there's nothing else here,' Nick mused. 'No seaside town, no funfair, no casino, no discos. Poor Katie. You're going to find it so dull.'

'Not me,' she said, so softly that he barely heard. He glanced at her. She was gazing over the empty land and beach with a curious little smile that was for herself alone.

'But there's nothing to do but ride and swim,' he pointed out. 'That's not going to be enough for a fun girl like you.'

'Don't worry,' she said, still with that little smile. 'There's plenty for me to do.'

She seemed to come out of a dream, and smiled at his puzzled face. 'Let's go to the beach,' she said. 'Come on. Last one at the stables is a sissy.'

Nick had meant to stay away only from Friday to Tuesday, but when he called Patsy on the cottage phone on Monday morning she said that he had no meetings this week, and she had everything under perfect control. Knowing her, he didn't doubt that this was true.

She told him about Lilian's visit. 'I should have called you earlier, but it went right out of my head.'

'And she couldn't call my mobile because it's been switched off. I found out ten minutes ago. I can't think how it happened.'

'You left here in such a rush, you probably did it by accident.'

'Do you think so?'

'Nothing else could possibly account for it,' Patsy said blandly.

He grinned. 'You've never liked Lilian, have you, Patsy?'

'I'm sure I don't know what you're talking about,' she retorted with lofty dignity, and hung up.

He supposed he ought to contact Lilian. They *were* practically engaged. He reached for the phone, then let his hand fall. There was no point in calling now. She was always busy on a Monday morning. But he knew that actually he was reluctant to endanger the fragile idyll that had enveloped him without his quite knowing how.

In the short time they'd been at Bay Cottage they'd bathed from the deserted cove, gone riding, and shared cosy evenings just chatting over a meal. Katie, whom he'd thought of as belonging with the bright lights, seemed completely happy.

A strange lassitude seemed to have come over him. It might have been the unaccustomed outdoor life, or it might have been the sudden release from work cares. Whatever the reason, he found himself constantly dozing on the beach, or yawning at ten o'clock in the evening.

One afternoon, as they headed for the sea after an energetic ride, he was startled to see Katie carrying a huge black umbrella that she'd found in the cottage.

'Whatever do you want that for?' he asked, grinning. 'It isn't going to rain.'

'Wait and see,' was all she would say.

As soon as they'd found their usual spot, she tossed her silk jacket onto the sand and stretched her arms up to the sun. She always did this, and Nick told himself he was used to it, but actually the sight affected him anew every time. He wished she would wear a respectable one-piece instead of the delicate bikinis. She seemed to have a new one each day. This one was peacock-blue, an exquisite shade against the gentle tan she was developing.

He tried not to look at her, but even with his face averted he was intensely aware of the shape of her hips and the way her breasts swelled beautifully against the scrap of material that covered them. He knew he must act quickly.

'Come on,' he said, heading for the sea without waiting for her.

In the water she acted like a mischievous puppy, diving and grabbing his legs, or vanishing without warning, only reappearing when she'd got him thoroughly worried.

'Little wretch!' he yelled when her head reappeared. 'Come here, Katie. You're too far out and the tide's turning.' As he spoke he could feel the tug of the outgoing tide against his legs. He reached for her, but she stepped back, enticing him on.

He took a few determined strides, seized hold of her outstretched hands, and pulled her towards him. At the same instant an incoming wave washed her forward and straight into his arms. He held onto her tightly, and was shockingly aware of her bare skin against his.

His head swam. He could feel the blood pounding in his veins and it was suddenly hard to breathe. Katie was clinging onto him, her arms around his neck.

'How silly of me,' she gasped. 'Thank you for saving me, Nick.'

'Nonsense,' he said roughly. 'You weren't in any real danger.'

'Not now you're here,' she said. 'Take me in to the shore.'

He fought his reactions down and carried her the rest of the way. Thank heavens she hadn't noticed, he thought.

They towelled themselves off and stretched out on the sand. Nick could still feel his heart thumping, and he knew he needed some time to sort himself out. He closed his eyes to prevent conversation. He couldn't bear to talk to Katie right now. Her very innocence was a reproach. The warmth seemed to wash over him, blurring his thoughts...

He awoke to find himself lying comfortably in the shade, with a blissful feeling of peace and well-being. He blinked, and realised that the shade was the large umbrella. Katie was holding it protectively, at an angle that must have made her arm ache. She smiled at him.

'Have you been holding that thing over me all the time?' he asked, touched.

'Not all the time. I started by resting it on the sand, but then the sun moved, so I had to move the umbrella. In the end I got tired of moving it, so I held it over you.'

'That's very sweet of you. This is what you brought it for?'

'Of course. You always go to sleep.'

'It comes from being so old and ancient,' he said, yawning.

'Stop putting yourself down. You're in your prime.'

'No, I'm not,' he said hastily, remembering that moment in the water. 'Into the sear and yellow, I promise you.'

She giggled, and the sound went up his spine.

'Look what I've got here,' she said, showing him the local paper. 'There's a funfair at Stavewell. Let's go. I love funfairs. Unless, of course, you're feeling too decrepit.'

'I think I could just about haul my aging bones over,' he said.

Over supper, he studied a local map and discovered that Stavewell was about twenty miles away. The Silent Monster would make nothing of it. Katie was ecstatic, like a child with her first treat. Nick regarded her tenderly, glad to have restored their relationship to a safe level.

But the next day something happened which made him wonder how well he'd ever known her.

CHAPTER NINE

THIER day out began badly. As they drove through the village the Silent Monster began making ominous noises, and within a few minutes it was juddering.

'I'm afraid we won't get there in this,' Nick observed. 'Sorry, Katie.'

'But we can still go to the funfair,' she said anxiously. 'There's a garage just along the road. When you've left the car there we can get the bus to Stavewell.'

'Go bouncing twenty miles over country roads in the local bus?' he said, aghast. 'The locals probably carry their chickens with them.'

'Oh, please, Nick,' she begged. 'It's the last day of the funfair, and I do so want to go.'

'All right,' he said indulgently. 'Just for you.'

'Do you really mean that?' she asked.

For a mad moment he wanted to say that he'd do anything in return for her sunny smile. He controlled himself quickly. 'I meant anything to stop you nagging me all day about this wretched funfair. We'll go. We may have to share a bus with a mass of livestock, or we may have to hitch-hike every step of the way, but we'll go.'

'That's all right, then,' she said contentedly. 'Only can we hurry? Because the bus goes in half an hour, and there isn't another one.'

Nick had misgivings about leaving his new car with a small country garage, but the owner pinpointed the problem without difficulty and promised to have it ready by evening.

They strolled casually towards the bus stop. Katie was looking stunning, he thought, in an orange shirt, bright yellow trousers and a matching yellow chiffon scarf holding back her hair. She hummed as she walked along, and gave the occasional skip.

'How old are you?' he teased.

'I just like funfairs,' she said airily. 'They bring out the kid in me.'

Then her smile faded, and she halted, looking around.

'What's that?' she said. 'Listen.'

Nick did so, and discerned the sound of wailing. Katie ran forward to a narrow alley that led between two shops. A toddler was there, running up and down the alley, sobbing her heart out.

'Mummy!' she called. 'Mummy...*Mummy!*' The last word was a scream of terror.

'Here, darling,' Katie cried, running towards the child and scooping her up. The child clasped her little arms tightly about Katie's neck and sobbed noisily.

'What can she be doing out here on her own?' Katie asked of Nick. 'Where's Mummy, pet?'

For answer, the child screamed again. She was shaking with distress, and Katie patted her back, trying to calm her down. She was a heavy child, and Katie was slightly built, but she seemed to bear the weight easily.

'Maybe she came out of the bakery,' Nick said, looking at a side door that led off the alley. 'Let's try.'

But inside the bakery nobody could offer them any help. Neither Dave, the baker, or his wife had ever seen the child before.

'She's not local,' Dave observed, 'or I'd know her. Perhaps we'd better call the police.'

'Let's hope they get here soon, or we'll miss that bus,' Nick reminded Katie in a low voice. She answered him with an abstracted smile, her attention on the child.

Luckily the local police station was just around the corner, and in a few minutes a smiling young police-woman appeared and introduced herself as Constable Jill Henson.

'Poor little soul,' she said. 'I wonder if she can tell us who she is.'

'What's your name, darling?' Katie asked softly.

The toddler hiccuped, and finally managed to whisper, 'Katie.'

'But that's my name, too,' Katie cried, sounding as delighted as if someone had given her a present. 'Fancy us both being Katie. What about your other name?'

But the child shook her head, while tears still rolled down her cheeks.

'Come on,' Katie encouraged her. 'I'll tell you mine if you'll tell me yours. Here goes. My last name is Deakins. Now it's your turn.'

But little Katie only looked at her miserably.

'Are you in a hurry, sir?' Jill Henson asked, seeing Nick check his watch.

'The bus is due any moment,' he said.

'You go and catch it, then. I'll take this little one back to the station. She'll be quite safe until we find her family.'

Jill put out her arms, but the child tightened her grip on Katie's neck and began to cry again.'

'I think she feels safer with me,' Katie said. 'I'm sorry, Nick, after I made such a fuss about it. But I can't leave her while she's like this.'

'Of course not,' he agreed. He was regarding Katie with wonder, noticing for the first time how large and capable her hands were compared to the rest of her. They might have been a mother's hands as she soothed the child and held her in a strong embrace.

'Poor baby,' she whispered. 'Poor little girl. Don't worry. We're going to find Mummy.'

Dave produced a sweet bun and a glass of milk. The child eyed them, her head resting against Katie's shoulder, one arm still tightly around her neck. Only when Katie offered her the milk did she consent to take a sip, and Katie had to feed her tidbits of cake.

As she calmed down she found it easier to remember, and hiccuped out a little more information. Her name was Katie Jensen, and, 'Mummy fell down.' But she couldn't tell them where it had happened.

'We'd better get back to the station,' Jill said. 'Then I can make some calls.'

As they walked along the High Street the bus to Stavewell passed them, stopped to collect passengers and went on out of sight. But Katie was absorbed in the little girl in her arms and didn't even notice.

The police force of Mainhurst numbered just three, and the station was just about big enough. They sat down on hard benches while Jill got on the phone.

The child had nodded off, seemingly content with her head on Katie's shoulder. Anyone would be content, Nick thought, held by those strong, comforting hands, and soothed by such a tender, womanly voice.

'I've found her,' Jill said, hanging up. 'Mrs Jensen collapsed in the street. Somebody came across her and called an ambulance, but they never mentioned a child, so she must have run off already. Mrs Jensen's in the County Hospital. Apparently it was just a dizzy spell, but she's going out of her mind with worry. I'll take the little girl over there.'

She regarded the sleeping child. 'I know it's a lot to ask,' she said to Katie, 'but would you mind coming with her?'

'I always meant to,' Katie said with a gentle smile.

It took half an hour to get to the County Hospital, where they found Mrs Jensen on her feet again. Her face wore a distracted look that vanished as soon as they entered. Little Katie awoke and held out her arms to her mother.

'I can hardly believe it,' she said, when she'd exclaimed and wept with relief, and her daughter was in her arms again. 'She never likes strangers, but she's really taken to you.'

'Ah, but we're both Katie, you see,' Katie said, smiling. 'That makes all the difference.' She beamed at the child. 'Doesn't it?'

Little Katie nodded vigorously and chuckled.

'You've been so kind,' Mrs Jensen said. 'Anybody might have found her, but not everyone would have cared for her the way you did. I hope it didn't put you out much.'

'Not at all,' Katie said warmly. 'We weren't doing anything today. I hope your illness isn't serious.'

'Oh, I'm not really ill.' She patted her stomach. 'I'm going to have another one, and it sort of caught up with me.' She hesitated, then said, 'I hope you have lots of children of your own. You were made to be a mother.'

Suddenly Katie blushed deeply. Nick had always known her to be mistress of every situation, but for the first time in his experience she seemed confused. He touched her shoulder, but to his surprise she turned away from him.

'We have to be going now,' Jill said. 'I'm glad it had a happy ending.'

Katie flicked the child's cheek softly, but little Katie threw out her arms and demanded to be taken up. Child and woman exchanged enthusiastic hugs. Mrs Jensen regarded them, misty-eyed.

'Your wife's a very special person,' she confided to Nick. 'You're a lucky man.'

'I——yes, I am,' he said awkwardly. He was watching Katie, who seemed enveloped in a golden glow.

Jill drove back to Mainhurst, but Nick and Katie opted to stay where they were and explore.

'Where to now?' Nick asked.

'Nick, I'm terribly sorry. I was such a pain about the funfair, and then I just let it go. You must be really fed up with me.'

'I wouldn't change one single thing about today,' he said, meaning it. 'You were wonderful.'

'What are we going to do now?' she asked. 'Your car won't be ready yet.'

At that moment Nick saw a bus approaching, with a notice on the front that said 'Mertley'. A mad impulse seized him.

'Let's get on that,' he said.

'But what is there in Mertley?'

'I've no idea.' He'd already grasped her hand and was running for the bus. They reached it just in time and tumbled onto the seats, laughing and embracing to steady each other.

'Where are you going, sir?' the conductor asked.

'Anywhere,' he said recklessly.

'This bus stops at Franchester, Wiggingham and Mertley.'

'Wherever. Two tickets to there.'

The conductor gave them two tickets to Mertley and edged away hastily.

'But we don't know anything about the place,' Katie protested.

'We'll find out when we get there—if we get there. We may go mad and get off at Franchester or Wiggingham. Let's live dangerously.'

'But you're normally such a methodical man,' she said in wonder.

'To hell with being methodical! I'm on holiday.'

The bus wound its way deep into the countryside, along roads that ran between high hedges. Then it breasted a hill and there was a panorama of trees and fields, laid out in the sunlight.

'This is Franchester,' the conductor said. He sounded hopeful, and he was rewarded, for his two crazy passengers promptly decided that here and nowhere else was the place they most wanted to be.

Franchester was a village, even tinier than Mainhurst. It had one shop that sold everything, and here Katie bought sandwiches, cream buns and soft drinks.

'What are you trying to do to my waistline?' Nick groaned.

'You'll have to go to the gym,' Katie teased, adding provocatively, 'if you can find the way.'

Nick enquired if there were any good picnic sites, and the man behind the counter directed them along the road.

'There's a public right of way over the field,' he said. 'And some very nice woods beyond.'

They thanked him and left. Further along they found a stile with a notice proclaiming a public footpath. The pressure of a thousand feet had left the path clearly marked, and they set off over the field, which formed an incline. At last they were high enough to see a gate on the far side, and a path leading straight to it. But they also saw something else.

'Nick,' Katie said nervously, 'they look awfully big to be cows.'

'But they're not bulls,' Nick said, with more confidence than he felt. 'At least, not exactly. They're steer. I've heard they're really quite gentle.'

'That one by the gate doesn't look gentle.'

They looked back the way they'd come, but the rest of the steer had drifted across the path.

'Twenty behind and one in front,' Katie said. 'They must be safe, or they wouldn't be in this field.'

'Unless it's the farmer's way of sending a message.'

They moved cautiously towards the steer ahead of them. He also moved, until he was right across the gate.

'We'll just have to defy him,' Nick said.

'Right,' she agreed, clasping his hand. 'Forward together!'

'Forward together!'

They advanced on the steer, looked him in the eyes, took deep breaths, and yelled, *'Boo!'*

The animal's reaction was instantaneous. He gave a deafening bellow of protest and scuttled away. Nick and Katie got through the gate as fast as they could.

'You see?' he said airily. 'I told you he was perfectly safe.'

'Sez you! You were as scared as I was.'

'More,' he assured her. 'More.'

The wood was an enchanted land, with widely spaced trees, good paths and a stream chuckling through it. They settled against a tree by the water and spread out their picnic. Nick eyed the cream buns and cherryade dubiously. It was the sort of thing he hadn't had since his teens, but it tasted delicious.

'Do you realise,' Katie mused, 'that right this minute not a soul in all the world knows where we are?'

'Yes,' he said contentedly. 'And that's just how I like
it.'

'What happened to the buccaneer of commerce?' she
teased.

'The buccaneer of commerce has still got his mobile
switched off,' he said contentedly. 'And it's staying that
way.'

'But you are happy about your new job, aren't you,
Nick?'

'I'm overwhelmed. I keep having to pinch myself to
believe this is happening to me. I never really saw myself up there.'

'Go on, you always had masses of self-confidence.
Cock o' the walk. That was you.'

He gave a wry smile. 'That was only on the surface.
I thought of myself as second-best.'

'Brian?' she hazarded.

'Was it that obvious?'

'No, I just guessed. Brian's a real knock-out. I expect
he was always gorgeous, right from the start.'

'Yes, he was,' Nick remembered. 'Even when we
were kids Mum's friends used to go misty-eyed about
him. Then they'd say, "Oh, yes, and Nick."' He
grinned. 'It made me so mad.

'But I was the brainy one. Brian, bless him, can never
remember anything between the covers of a book. So I
studied hard and came top of the class. I wanted the
satisfaction of having him jealous of me for a change.'

'I can't imagine Brian being jealous.'

'You're right. He was madly proud of me, and when
I won something on school prize day he led the applause.'

'He must be the sweetest-natured man on earth,' Katie
reflected.

'He won a prize too, that day, as captain of the football team. And when he went up to get it the whole school went mad. You've never heard cheering like it. They loved him, you see. I realised then that that was his real gift, and it was useless trying to compete with it.'

'Did you really understand that?' Katie said thoughtfully. 'Didn't you actually go on competing with him?'

'Yes, and he won every time.' Nick relapsed into silence, but Isobel's name seemed to hang in the air between them. 'He wasn't competing, you see. He never knew it was a competition.'

'Does it matter so much?' Katie asked softly. 'Couldn't you let go now?'

'I don't know if I can. I've got so used to thinking in that confined space in my head—although right now it seems...' He hesitated, trying to find the words.

But then he knew the words didn't matter. Katie understood. The eyes in her pixie face were those of a wise woman, and her smile was as comforting as the one she'd given the child.

He began to talk, and for once he wasn't thinking about the words before he said them. Out they poured, a spontaneous release of things he'd never told another living soul, fears he'd been ashamed to admit, and feelings he hadn't wanted to examine, like his guilt for the injustice he'd always done his brother.

Katie knew how to listen, letting him work out his own train of thought without interrupting, except to ask a question full of empathy. He knew her mind was in perfect tune with his, and the knowledge was like a liberation.

Suddenly it was there again, the intangible 'something' that she had in common with Isobel. He wondered if this was the answer, because Isobel was also sympathetic and easy to talk to. It made sense, yet there was still the elusive sense of something else...a mystery still to be revealed...

'Nick, what's wrong?'

'Nothing. I was just musing. It'll come to me.'

'What will?'

'Never mind.' He gave a grunt of laughter. 'Just look at us, talking like this. Remember how we used to be?'

'At daggers drawn.'

'Why were you so agin me, Katie? I've always wondered. I thought once that you didn't want Isobel to marry *anyone*, but you liked Brian. And your idea of fun was to spread banana skins for me.'

She chuckled. 'You never saw them until it was too late. It was so tempting. But I was a horrid brat, wasn't I?'

'I thought so, especially that day you dropped a spider down my back.'

'And you hauled it out and dropped it down *my* back,' she recalled, with feeling.

'And you squealed the place down.'

'You were rotten!'

'You asked for it! I'd just like to know why you disliked me so much?'

'I didn't—not really. But you were so lofty. Katie the Kid was beneath your notice.'

He groaned. 'Patsy was right. She said men get pompous at twenty-four because they feel entitled to respect. You never gave me any of that.'

'Poor Nick,' she said, her eyes tender and mischievous. 'I was going through an awkward stage, and I took it all out on you.'

'Can't think why you bothered. If you were sixteen you should have been out with boyfriends.'

'The way I looked?' she asked hilariously.

'You weren't so bad.'

'I looked like a stick insect in a dress. Oh, and I did so want to be beautiful! I used to dream about having a voluptuous figure.' She outlined a huge bosom and vast hips over her delicate shape. 'And then all the boys would chase me. But they just treated me like one of the lads.'

'Well, that's changed, at least.'

'Yes, I suppose I'm all right now.'

'Stop fishing,' he said with a grin. 'You know you're a knock-out.'

For answer, she just smiled at him. It was a glorious, dizzying smile, and it made him understand why Ratchett couldn't stop following her. The thought reminded him of something.

'Katie, you know why I've brought you away, don't you?'

'To have a vacation?'

'That too, but something else—something we've put off discussing for too long.'

'Yes, Nick?' He was too preoccupied watching the way the light slanted through the trees onto her hair to notice that her voice was breathless with hope.

'I wanted to get you well away from Jake Ratchett while we decide what to do about him.'

'Jake?' she echoed faintly. 'You mean, that's why—?'

'Yes. Although sometimes I wonder if I did the right thing. It might have been better for me to confront him, and show him that you aren't alone. But then we'd have missed all this, and that would have been a pity. Ratchett can wait, for now, but some day soon I'll have to deal with him.'

Katie looked awkward. 'Please, I don't want to talk about Jake just now.'

'Of course you don't. We came here to forget him.' He took her hand. 'Don't look like that, Katie. I'm here to look after you.'

'I know you are,' she said softly, and squeezed his hand.

He looked at his watch and exclaimed, 'Look at the time! When's the last bus?'

'I never thought to ask.'

'Typical!'

'Well, you didn't think to ask either,' she said indignantly.

'What's that got to do with it?' he demanded, with impeccable male logic.

Hand in hand, they hurried back through the field, regarded impassively by the herd of steer. They reached the stop just in time to see the bus vanishing around the next corner.

A check in the shop revealed that they'd missed the last bus of the day, and that the only taxi in town was out.

'Come on,' Nick said, putting his arm around her shoulder.

'What are we going to do?'

'Walk?'

They'd trudged a mile before a buzzing sound came from far behind them. It was dark now, and all they could see was a pair of headlamps getting steadily closer.

'It's a truck, by the size of it,' Nick said. 'We might be in luck.'

They were. The truck, which was loaded with hay,

slowed in response to their frantic waving and a man's head popped out of the window. He was middle-aged and friendly. 'Missed the last bus, eh?'

His road lay within a couple of hundred yards of the cottage and they gladly accepted his offer to ''op on the back'. They climbed up and threw themselves down on the sweet-smelling hay with sighs of relief.

'I'll have to get the car tomorrow,' Nick said with a yawn.

There was so much he wanted to say, but he couldn't find the words. Instead he took her hand in his and they lay back on the hay in silence, looking up at the winking stars while the truck bumped its way along the road.

By the time the driver dropped them off the moon was out and they could see the cottage in the distance. They thanked him and set off on the walk.

The cottage had never looked so welcoming. They were both worn out after the long day. Nick made cocoa and Katie accepted it with a yawn and a smile. He smiled back in deep contentment.

'Katie…' he said as she headed for the stairs.

'Yes?'

'Nothing,' he said after a moment. 'Just—goodnight.'

He wanted to be alone to sort out his confused thoughts. Today he'd seen so many different sides of Katie that his head was in a whirl. She was never the same person from one minute to the next, and he couldn't keep up.

Once she'd been the brat who'd made his life a bed of nails. But the years had wondrously transformed her into a woman who was not only beautiful, but someone to whom he could confide his deepest thoughts. He went to sleep thinking how curiously life turned out.

But he was about to discover that the Poison Pixie still lived!

CHAPTER TEN

NICK rose early, and found the day so glorious that he rejected a taxi in favour of walking to Mainhurst. Putting his head tentatively around Katie's door, he found her dead to the world, and backed out. After scribbling her a note he set off for the village, where he found the car working properly again.

On his return to the cottage he found that it was Katie's turn to disappear. Her note said that she'd gone for a ride, and invited him to join her. He made himself a quick snack and was just about to leave when there was a knock at the door. Opening it, he found a young woman bearing a huge bouquet of red roses.

'Special delivery for Miss Deakins.'

'Fine, I'll take them,' he said, puzzled.

As he set the roses on the table a card fell out. It bore the logo of the Redmond Hotel, in the town of Chockley, about twenty miles away. Nick felt a familiar anger rise from the pit of his stomach as he read. *Wherever you go, I'll always find you. J.R.*

'My God, he's even got his spies checking her movements,' he seethed. 'Well, this is where it ends. I'm not having her alarmed. It's time Mr Ratchett and I had a few words.'

He tossed the huge bouquet into the back of the car and headed for Chockley. The Redmond was the most expensive hotel for miles, set in its own grounds and exuding an air of blatant luxury. Just the sort of place

Ratchett would be bound to choose, Nick decided furiously.

He marched up to the desk, bearing the bouquet. 'Which is Mr Ratchett's room?' he demanded.

He was uncomfortably aware of the receptionist's look of astonishment. Too late he realised the impression he must be giving, clutching the roses. He scowled, notching this up as another black mark against Ratchett.

'Mr Ratchett has a suite of rooms on the first floor,' the young woman said. 'Perhaps his secretary could—?'

'No, thank you. I want Ratchett himself.' As he turned away he noted, out of the corner of his eye, that the receptionist had picked up the phone.

He climbed the stairs two at a time and rapped sharply on the door. It was opened at once by a tall, thin young man with an air of apprehension. Nick pushed past him into the room and tossed the roses onto a table.

'I see your boss isn't man enough to face me himself,' he snapped. 'But sending you in his place isn't going to help him. Tell him I'm not leaving until he comes out of hiding.'

The young man gulped. 'I—I beg your pardon?'

He had an Australian accent, and a deep voice that was incongruous against his timid-looking person. With a sense of shock Nick remembered where he'd heard that voice before…

'*You're* Jake Ratchett?' he said, thunderstruck.

'Why, yes, I—I don't know why you should think I wasn't.'

'The receptionist mentioned a secretary—'

'They found me a local temp. I have to work wherever I go. My dad's a hard taskmaster.' The young man looked at the flowers in anguish. 'I guess Katie didn't like them. Was she offended because they're red roses?

Oh, gosh, yes! She thought I was presuming. I should have made them white—or maybe chrysanthemums—only she doesn't like chrysanthemums.'

Nick's brain was reeling. This diffident boy surely couldn't be Jake Ratchett, the grim pursuer of his nightmares?

'I think we have some talking to do,' he said.

'Would you like a drink?' Jake offered politely.

'Coffee, please. Black and very sweet. I'm in deep shock.'

Jake called Room Service, and there was just a hint of the person Nick had expected to find. This was a rich young man, who knew that his wants would be catered for instantly. But nothing else fitted the picture. Jake's eyes were large and brown, like an eager puppy's, and his tone was placating.

'Katie must be really angry to send my flowers back,' he sighed.

'Katie hasn't seen them. I'm the one who's annoyed. I came to tell you to leave her alone and stop following her around the world. It alarms and upsets her.'

'I didn't know that,' Jake said, looking horrified. 'She's never seemed scared. Mostly she just laughs at me. I've really tried to be the kind of man she wants...'

'Look,' Nick said distractedly, 'there seems to have been some— By the way, my name's Nick Kenton.'

Jake shook his hand respectfully. 'I've been looking forward to meeting you, Mr Kenton.'

'You know about me?'

'Only what Katie's told me—about you being her sister's brother-in-law and looking after her while she's here.'

The coffee arrived, and Jake acted as 'mother'. He

seemed naturally domesticated, and Nick's prejudices took another knock.

'You just can't be the man I've been talking to,' he said, dazed. 'That fellow's a tyrant who barks orders, and you're—' He broke off tactfully, and regarded Jake's unimpressive person.

'I can only do it on the phone,' Jake explained. 'If folks see me they fall about laughing, so when they can't see me I kind of—make up for it. Have I been overdoing that?'

'Definitely.'

'Oh, dear! I'm sorry. Look, never mind me. Is Katie all right?'

'She's fine. She was out riding when I left.'

'But you said she's upset. Is someone with her, in case she has a fall?'

Nick looked at him with sympathy. 'She's really got you jumping through hoops, hasn't she?'

Jake's smile was warm and delightful. 'Everyone jumps through hoops for Katie,' he said simply. 'She's that kind of girl. She can make you feel that anything you do for her is worth it.'

'And doesn't she know it!' Nick murmured.

'You too?'

'No,' he said hastily. 'At least, she's had me jumping through a few hoops, but that's because she enjoys giving me a hard time. It's her hobby.'

'That's not a very nice thing to say about her,' Jake said, sounding shocked. 'You make her sound heartless.'

'She rides roughshod over me and enjoys doing it.'

Nick had spoken jokingly, but there was no humour in Jake's response. 'I'm sure you're mistaken about that, sir. Katie is the most sweet, generous, kindly—'

'She's all those things,' Nick interrupted hastily. 'But

she's also a sharp-witted, conniving little shrew. Look, I'm not criticising her. I'm just explaining that I'm not in love with her.'

'You're not?' Jake sounded amazed.

'Not every man in the world is in love with Katie. It just seems that way.'

'All the ones I know are.'

'Well, maybe you shouldn't make it so obvious. Instead of laying yourself at her feet, why not try fanning her interest by being hard to get?'

'But she doesn't want to "get" me,' Jake said despondently. 'How can you fan an interest that doesn't exist?'

This was so unanswerable that Nick could only drain his coffee. Jake immediately poured him another with solicitous care.

'Aren't you having any coffee?'

'Thank you, sir, but I never touch stimulants. But I do feel in need of something.' He opened the fridge and poured himself a glass of mineral water.

'You seem pretty well taken care of,' Nick said, indicating the well-stocked fridge.

'My favourite yoghurt isn't available in this country, so I travel with a supply,' Jake explained. 'But this hotel has been really good about finding me some low-fat cheese.' He saw Nick's glassy-eyed gaze, and misunderstood. 'I guess I'm a little extravagant.'

'Not at all,' Nick said. By now he was in a fog.

'Sir—'

'I wish you'd stop calling me sir,' Nick said tensely. 'It makes me feel a hundred.'

'I'm sorry. It's just that while Katie's in England I look on you as her father—'

'Oh, *do* you? Then let me put you right. A merciful providence spared me that burden at least.'

'No, I only meant that as you're so much older—'

'I'm twenty-nine,' Nick said in a tight voice.

Jake tore his hair. 'I'm making a mess of this,' he said unnecessarily. 'I'm talking about you as a father *figure*, a—a voice of authority that she might listen to—'

'Jake, I'm beginning to feel sorry for you. Let me warn you not to talk about my "authority" to Katie. She's liable to kick your shins—or mine.'

'She's got plenty of spirit, hasn't she?' Jake said eagerly.

'You can say that again!'

'It's what makes her so thrilling to be with.'

'It makes her exhausting to be with,' Nick said gloomily. 'Whatever are you about, to let her walk over you like this? Following her from Australia was a terrible idea. Do you want to drive her crazy with power?'

'I didn't actually come to England just because of Katie. My dad has business over here that someone had to see to.' Jake looked sheepish. 'But I admit I volunteered.'

'You really are a glutton for punishment. How did you know about the cottage?'

'I followed you when you drove down. It wasn't easy to stay just the right distance behind, but I managed it.'

Nick regarded him with sympathy. 'How old are you, Jake?'

'Twenty-four.'

'Take my advice and forget her. She's too much for you to cope with.'

'I'm sorry, sir, but you just don't understand how I feel.'

'Yes, I do,' Nick said gently. 'I was twenty-four once, and in love with a woman that I thought— Well, anyway, I tried to be the kind of person I thought she'd like me to be. And in the end—' he gave a brief, rueful laugh '—I lost her to a man who won her heart with a smile.'

'But—but surely a woman appreciates a man who tries to improve himself for her sake?' Jake sounded shocked.

'Of course, but it's no good if that's all there is. The spark has to be there. The magic. And if it isn't, anything else is a waste of time. You can't fall in love with someone just because they love you, any more than you can stop loving them because they don't love you.'

And you couldn't, he thought, fall in love with a woman just because she was elegant and sophisticated and a suitable wife. If the spark wasn't there you would find yourself dreaming of another woman, an impish female with laughing eyes and a wicked sense of fun. Because she was magic. She was maddening and infuriating. She could make you want to climb the walls. You could tear your hair and curse the day you'd met her. But she was magic.

'Why don't you have dinner with us tonight?' he said.

Jake's face shone with delight. 'I can see Katie? You really mean it?'

'So much perseverance deserves a reward. But it's time you started getting her out of your system. You're much too good for her.'

'No man's good enough for Katie,' the boy said fervently.

'Jake, you're a nice fellow, but when you talk that way I want to throw up. Katie is not a divine goddess. She's a harpy, a witch, a Poison Pixie. I could go insane just thinking about her.'

'Yes, sir, she's really unforgettable, isn't she?'

He groaned. 'There's no hope for you. All right, put

that bouquet back in water and you can give it to her tonight.'

'Give Katie stale flowers?' Jake echoed, in a tone that implied Nick had suggested something indecent. 'I'll buy new ones—the best I can get.'

He was past praying for, Nick decided.

Katie returned in the late afternoon. She'd ridden further than she'd meant and found herself lost.

There was no sign of Nick, but the sight that met her eyes made her stop and stare. In the centre of the room stood a table laid for two. The cottage's best china had been lovingly washed and arranged. Tall, sparkling glasses stood beside each plate, set off by snowy napkins. Delicious smells wafted from the kitchen, and she could hear the sound of Nick humming.

A slow smile, brilliant with joy, spread over Katie's face. Her eyes shone as she took in every detail of the table, lovingly prepared so that two people could enjoy a romantic evening.

'Nick,' she called eagerly, heading for the kitchen. *'Nick—'*

He met her in the doorway, a salad bowl in one hand and a large spoon in the other. He'd fixed a teatowel through his belt as an apron.

'So there you are,' he said sternly.

'Yes, I'm sorry I'm late. I got lost. Oh, Nick, if I'd known you were thinking of anything like this—'

'I didn't know myself until a few hours ago,' he said, setting down the salad bowl and spoon. 'But then something happened that changed everything.'

'Yes?' she asked eagerly.

'I met Jake Ratchett,' he said, regarding her steadily.

Katie grew pale. 'You met—Jake?'

'He sent you a huge bouquet of red roses. I got mad
for your sake—which was silly of me, knowing you—
and took it back to him.' He crossed his arms and gave
her a challenging look.

For once he had the satisfaction of seeing Katie
Deakins lost for words. Various expressions flitted
across her face, but the one that settled there was guilt.

'I don't know how you can look me in the eyes,' he
said. 'Jake Ratchett is just a poor, dumb kid who, for
reasons that are a mystery to me, thinks you're wonderful. I went there expecting a monster—'

'I never told you he was a monster,' Katie broke in
quickly.

'Maybe not in words, but you contrived to let me
think it. Of all the unscrupulous, unprincipled...' Words
failed him. 'I was going to ask you why you did it,' he
resumed at last, 'but actually I know exactly why.'

'You do?' she asked breathlessly.

'Of course. It's part of your usual game of "Let's
make a fool of Nick and have a good laugh". Well,
tonight the laugh's going to be on you. I've invited him
to dinner.'

'You mean—all this is for him?' she faltered, indicating the table.

'That's right. You're going to entertain Jake Ratchett,
and be very, very nice to him. You owe the poor mutt
that much. You'll receive his bouquet with delight—it'll
be a new one, since he wouldn't dream of insulting you
with this morning's flowers—and you'll give him your
undivided attention for the whole evening.'

'But what about you?' she asked, looking at the two
places.

'I shall be in the local tavern,' he informed her firmly,
'chatting up the barmaid.'

*   *   *

Jake arrived by taxi, explaining that he'd loaned his car to his secretary. From his harassed look, Nick guessed that he hadn't meant to do that, but that the secretary knew a soft-hearted sucker when she saw one.

Nick had looked forward to their meeting with interest, but if he'd expected Katie to be awkward he'd underestimated her. She'd taken special care over her appearance, and looked so ravishingly pretty that Nick was reluctant to leave them alone together. But he was committed now.

Perhaps it was guilt that made her greet Jake warmly, or a kind-hearted desire to make amends. The boy was in seventh heaven, especially seeing the care that had been taken at the elegantly laid table.

'You shouldn't have gone to all this trouble,' he told her, and Katie had the grace to blush.

Satisfied that he'd left Jake in gentle hands, Nick drove off, promising to return later and drive Jake home. He was quite proud of that touch. It sounded properly paternal.

Jake's evening was straight out of heaven. Katie's kind-heartedness took over and made her spoil him. Nick had prepared a splendid vegetarian meal, and she served it, all smiles.

Some of his delight vanished later, though, when she gave him back his pendant.

'I can't accept it, Jake. It's very sweet of you, but it's much too expensive.'

'Please,' he begged, 'keep it as a goodbye present. I know the truth now.'

'Do you?' she asked quickly.

'I've been kidding myself, and pestering you. I won't do it any more.'

'Oh, Jake,' she said, clasping his hands, tears of sympathy in her eyes.

'Keep it, please,' he said, pressing the pendant into her hand. 'It would make me happy to think you were wearing it some time, and maybe thinking of me kindly.'

'I'll always think of you kindly,' she said sincerely. 'But I'll keep it if you like.' She slipped it on.

'I had a long talk with Nick today, and it made me see things more clearly.'

'I suppose he called me rude names?' Katie said with a smile.

'One or two, but that's just how he talks. Underneath, I think— Well...'

'Yes?' she asked, in the same breathless voice as before.

'Well—I think he's really quite fond of you, in a fatherly sort of way.'

'Yes, he is,' she said wryly.

'He was very kind. He told me he knew how I felt, because of a woman he was in love with when he was twenty-four, and he lost her.'

'That's my sister, Isobel. She married his brother.'

'Well, I guess he's still pretty stuck on her.'

'Did he say so?' Katie asked, not looking at him.

'Not in so many words, but he talked like she was the one and only woman. He said something about magic— how if the magic wasn't there, nothing else did any good, and you couldn't stop loving someone just because they didn't love you.'

'No,' Katie said with a soft little sigh. 'You can't.'

Nick returned three hours later, and looked from one to the other. At any rate there'd been no emotional storms, he thought.

'I'll wait for you in the car,' he said kindly to Jake, and left them alone.

Jake looked sadly at his goddess, his look of a confiding puppy more pronounced than ever. 'Don't worry, Katie. I won't bother you any more.'

'I wish I could fall in love with you, Jake. I would if I could.'

'But you're in love with this other guy, aren't you?'

'Who?' Katie demanded quickly.

'I don't know his name, but I've always guessed there was someone. All those guys you had hanging around you—and you flirted with them, but you were never really there. It was like your heart was with someone else. It's true, isn't it?'

'Yes, it's true,' Katie admitted. 'I've tried not to love him—tried for ages and ages—but it's no use.' She closed her eyes and a tear rolled down her cheek. 'Oh, Jake, it's terrible to love someone so much that it hurts, and they don't care about you at all.'

'I know,' he said gently.

She gave him a wonky smile. 'Yes, of course you do. I've been rotten to you. I'm so sorry.'

'Don't be. At least I've had this evening.'

'Yes, we both live on crumbs, and make the most of them. And when you know crumbs are all you're ever going to have…'

'Don't cry,' he said, taking her in his arms and urging her head onto his shoulder. 'Maybe it'll work out for you.'

'Maybe,' she said with a little laugh. 'Maybe pigs will fly.'

''Course they will. You'll make 'em fly.'

Jake mused dreamily about Katie all through the journey, and Nick bore it pretty well. He liked Jake, but he was beginning to find his company a bit lacking in variety. It wasn't until they turned into the hotel drive that Jake dropped his bombshell.

'I guess that secretly I always knew I didn't have a chance against the man Katie's in love with. I expect you know all about him?'

'Not a thing,' Nick said, startled. 'She's told you?'

'A little. Not much. I think it's someone she met in Australia, before me.'

'Or maybe someone since?'

'No, she's known him quite a while. She's really tried to get him out of her heart, but it didn't work. He must have treated her pretty badly, but she's still carrying a torch for him. I thought you'd know.'

'No,' Nick said in a hollow voice. 'I had no idea Katie was in love.'

'Nobody else stands a chance.' Jake gave a long sigh. 'It's kind of discouraging, isn't it?'

'Yes,' Nick murmured.

'She talked about him a little tonight. She was crying. That's how much he's hurt her. How can he be so stupid? Being loved by Katie would be the most wonderful thing in the world, and he—well, I just don't know.'

Luckily they'd reached the hotel door, and Nick was able to avoid answering. He deposited his passenger, bid him a kindly farewell and drove away, a mass of confused emotion.

Uppermost was a feeling of shock. He and Katie had seemed so close recently. He would have sworn that she'd confided everything to him, and the feeling had been delightful. Now it seemed that she'd concealed the deepest secrets of her heart. He didn't want to examine the feeling that was churning his stomach. It was too much like jealousy.

He couldn't go home like this, and talk and pretend

that everything was all right. He needed time to sort himself out before he faced Katie. He turned the car away from the cottage and drove off into the night. After an hour he reached a high peak, overlooking the sea. He got out and sat, listening to the crash of the waves below, trying to calm his turmoil.

Katie, in love! Not just in love, but in the grip of one of those persistent, unreasonable passions that turned the world upside down. For so long he'd thought of her as little more than a child, but she was a woman, with a vibrant, loving heart that she'd given to someone else.

And it was only at that moment that Nick faced how much he wanted her to give her heart to him. Suddenly he couldn't imagine life without her. If she were to go now, he would be desolate.

And this other man, this blind fool who was too proud or stupid to understand the treasure he'd won—suppose he turned up and carried her off?

With sudden resolution, Nick leapt back into the car and drove purposefully back home, as if afraid that she might have vanished in his absence. The cottage was in darkness, and he thought she must have gone to bed. But when he entered quietly he saw her sitting on the floor by the log fire. She'd changed into a kaftan made of some soft material and decorated in exotic colours, and her lovely hair flowed freely over her shoulders. The soft glow of the flickering flames lit up the glisten of tears on her cheeks.

She didn't hear Nick come in. She was too far lost in some dream of her own. For a moment he wondered if he should creep upstairs without disturbing her. But he stayed rooted to the spot, watching the golden light play across her enchanting face.

She sighed and rested her chin on her hands, which

lay on her knees. She was thinking of *him*, Nick realised, and the wistful yearning on her face confirmed everything Jake had said. This was no ordinary love. It had survived time and indifference, clinging on with despairing fidelity when hope was gone.

There was an ache in his heart. She was so near, and yet so far away. He wanted to say something, but he could only stand there, looking at her dumbly, overwhelmed with longing.

CHAPTER ELEVEN

KATIE glanced up quickly and passed a hand swiftly over her face to wipe away the tears.

'Hallo, Nick,' she said brightly. 'I didn't hear you come in. Shall I get you something?'

'No, stay there. I'll get it.'

There was still some wine on the table. He got two clean glasses and joined her on the floor.

'Did you get anywhere with the barmaid?' she asked.

'Who? Oh, the barmaid. No, she turned out to have an eight-foot husband with a karate black belt, so I thought better of it.' They exchanged smiles. 'I didn't really mean to chat up the barmaid. I spent the evening working on some figures.'

'Poor Nick. You should have been here with us.'

'I thought about you both, though, wondering how you were getting on. Did you let him down lightly?'

'Yes, he was ever so nice.'

'That's because he's still in love with you. He thinks everything you do is perfect.'

Her eyes teased him over the rim of the wine glass. 'Then he's the opposite of you. You think everything I do is a major crime, and you never forgive me for a thing.'

'Well—at one time, maybe. But not now I've come to understand why you did it.'

'Understand?' she asked breathlessly.

'I know you've been unhappy, and now I know why.

You should have told me about it before. It kind of hurts that you didn't.'

Katie prodded the burning wood. 'How much—how much do you know?'

'Jake told me a little, but I guessed some for myself. Suddenly everything fell into place. How I could have lived close to you all these weeks without seeing what was under my nose, I can't imagine. Oh, Katie, you should have told me.'

Her eyes were wide with wonder, as though she couldn't believe what she was hearing. 'Would you have wanted to know?' she whispered.

'Of course. We've had our spats, but I thought you trusted me. You could tell me anything—especially this.'

She set down the glass and looked back into the flames. She seemed suddenly awkward. 'It's not something you can just come out with,' she murmured.

He stroked her hair consolingly. 'I know. It's never easy to speak of things that are deep in your heart, but sometimes we should find the courage.'

She turned her head so that her cheek brushed against his hand. She was as lovely as a flower, and he wanted to kiss her there and then. But he forced himself not to. Katie needed comfort and friendship, not the tide of emotion that he longed to lavish on her.

'I wonder what you would have said,' she mused. 'I was afraid to embarrass you.'

'You wouldn't have embarrassed me. I'm your friend, remember. Tell me everything now, Katie.'

'Oh, Nick…'

She raised her face, and he saw it shining. How could she glow in such a way for the swine who'd ill-treated her? he thought jealously. For a moment his feelings almost broke through, but he forced himself back into the role of friend.

'I want to know all about this man,' he said.

She tensed. 'What?'

'This man you met in Australia—the one you've been in love with all this time. You told Jake about him.'

Before his eyes the light went out of her face, leaving a strangely bleak look. 'But you said you'd guessed the rest.'

'Well, yes, I guessed a bit. You must have met him soon after you went out there, and I think you came back here to forget him. And then you found you couldn't. Poor Katie.'

A tremor went through her, and for a moment she covered her eyes with her hand. 'I'll never forget him,' she said huskily. 'Never get over him.'

'At your age? Of course you will. There's plenty of time for the right man to come along.'

'But he *is* the right man. I knew that from the first moment. And when you've met the right one, that's it. There's nothing you can do about it. You just have to accept your fate.'

The melodramatic phrase reminded him of the old Katie, and he smiled.

'Don't laugh at me,' she said passionately.

'I wasn't. I was just remembering you when you were a kid, always so intense. Everything was life and death.'

'But some things really are life and death. Can't you see that?'

'Hey, calm down. Tell me what happened. What's his name?'

But she shook her head. 'No names. But I've loved him from the moment we met. I knew he was the one.'

'But you can't have been much more than a kid.'

'That didn't matter. He was special. It's not reasonable or logical. Your heart decides it.'

'Yes,' he murmured, looking at her in the firelight. 'Your heart decides it.'

She raised her eyes quickly, then looked away, as though there was something she couldn't bear to see.

'You were always impulsive—' he started to say, but she interrupted.

'No, it was more than that. I just knew.'

'Love at first sight,' he said sympathetically. 'But it doesn't last, Katie. It's built on illusion, and it fades with reality.'

'Yours didn't. You fell in love with Isobel at first sight, and it didn't fade even when she married your brother.'

'I don't think we should discuss her,' he said uneasily. He was feeling awkward about Isobel at this moment.

'No, of course. But you understand.'

'Did you get the chance to know him well?' he asked, trying to get off the subject of Isobel.

'Not really. We used to argue a lot. That was the only time he ever noticed me.'

'It doesn't sound as though he ever made you happy.'

A faint smile hovered on her lips. It was full of sadness, yet with a haunting echo of happiness remembered, or perhaps only longed for and never known.

'I was happy just being with him,' she said simply. 'And for the rest—I could always dream.' Her voice trembled. 'But he's never—he's never—'

Suddenly she broke down, burying her face in her hands and weeping desperately.

'Katie!' he said in dismay. 'Please don't.'

'I can't help it,' she sobbed. 'He'll never love me; I know he won't.'

'Then he's a fool,' he said, gathering her into his arms. 'Don't cry, Katie. Nothing's as bad as that.'

'I can't live on dreams any more, but they're all I can ever have. Oh, Nick, it hurts so much—'

Her grief went through him, breaking his heart as though the pain was his own. He held her tighter, caressing her hair, murmuring words of consolation.

'Don't, Katie, please,' he begged. 'It'll be all right one day…one day—'

'It won't, it won't,' she wept frantically. 'I've been so stupid. I thought I could make him love me, but he never will…'

He was filled with confusion. He'd seen Katie sparkling with merriment or anger, and he'd seen her tired, but never before had he seen her radiant spirit brought down. Tenderness streamed through him. He wanted to protect her from every wind that blew. If her unknown beloved had walked in Nick would have ordered him to love Katie on pain of dire retribution.

'I'm here,' he whispered. 'I know I'm not the one you want, but I'm here for you, Katie.'

He rocked her back and forth, murmuring soothingly, and gradually she grew calmer. 'Hold me, Nick,' she whispered. 'Just for a little while.'

'Of course I will, darling.' He hadn't mean to say 'darling', but it had slipped out. Luckily she wasn't offended. She clung to him as if he were her last hope, and he dropped his head to kiss her shining hair.

He didn't know how it happened. Perhaps she raised her face at the very same moment, but somehow their lips brushed together. Instead of moving away, she grew still. Nick knew he should disengage himself, but no power on earth could have made him do it while he was filled with such joy. Through the thin material he could

feel her slim young body. She was trembling as she lay
there in his arms, and then he realised that he too was
trembling.

He moved his lips over hers, caressing her mouth tenderly, pervaded by her sweetness. At first he wasn't sure
what she would do, but suddenly her arms were around
his neck and she was kissing him back.

He didn't know what was happening to him, what
madness had seized him. He only knew that this was the
most shatteringly beautiful moment he'd ever known. He
kissed her lips and they were honey.

His conscience smote him. This shouldn't be happening. But he was helpless in the grip of the desire that
flooded him. The only thing that could stop him now
was her own refusal, but instead of refusing she lay in
his arms, regarding him with a kind of wonder. Nor did
she protest when he undid the fastening of her loose
garment, exposing her breasts to his kisses.

He caressed them reverently with his lips and his
tongue, rejoicing in the response he could sense. She was
warm and inviting, and before he knew what he was
doing he'd pushed the kaftan down her body and ripped
open his own shirt.

Now he knew how much he'd wanted to be naked
with her. As they lay together on the great cushions he
was swept with desire, with love, and the urge to make
her his for all time. Her lips responded eagerly to his
deepening kisses, and her whole beautiful body was
aflame.

He felt her hands caressing him, tentatively at first, as
though she couldn't believe what was happening, but
then as though she enjoyed exploring him. She stroked
his smooth skin, kissing it between caresses, sometimes
stopping to look up at him with a little wondering smile.

The innocence in her eyes filled him with awe. His movements grew more tender, and infinitely gentle, as though her delicate beauty might break.

'Are you all right?' he whispered.

He wasn't sure if she heard him. Her only reply was a soft murmur. 'Nick…Nick…'

'Hold on to me, darling.'

As he moved towards their complete union she was there, waiting for him, as though this was something she wanted. Her arms were about his neck as he made her his own, and he heard her soft sigh.

She smelt of woodsmoke and wild berries, and she tasted of milk and honey. Despite her innocence she was as natural and sensual as a young animal, revelling in his skin, drinking in his aroma with long sighs of pleasure.

She responded to his ardour with every part of her, not just her arms and legs, but with her delicate fingers, her skin, her breath, her wonderful eyes. He said her name, dazed and incredulous at the miracle that had been given to him.

'Katie,' he murmured adoringly. 'Katie…Katie…'

She didn't say his name in return, but she kissed him passionately and drew him closer. When their moment came it was a true union. He put all his heart into it, and felt her trembling response.

Afterwards he felt sleep claim him almost at once. Lying there with Katie in his arms, her head resting on his chest, he knew that he'd come home. Her heart was close enough to his for him to know that its pounding rhythm was slowing in time to his own. She was his and he was hers, and nothing else mattered in life.

But when he slept, Isobel was there in his dreams, accusing him. She'd asked him to protect her young sister, and instead he'd taken advantage of Katie's youth and innocence. Worse, he'd seduced her when he'd known she didn't love him. His only excuse was that his feelings had swept over him. He was covered with shame.

'I'm sorry,' he told her. 'I'm sorry, Isobel.'

Then something became clear to him. He wasn't really apologising for betraying Isobel's trust, but for the fact that Katie had dislodged her in his heart. Katie was his true love, and there was no room for any other woman.

'I'm sorry, Isobel,' he said again. 'I'm so sorry.'

Katie didn't sleep at all. She lay against him, trying to come to terms with what had happened. When Nick stirred, she held him closer. When she heard him murmuring in his sleep she listened with her heart.

'I'm sorry, Isobel,' he whispered. 'I'm so sorry.'

After a long moment of total stillness Katie quietly moved away from him and put a distance between them. She lay for a while, staring into the darkness, while the tears flowed down her cheeks. But at last she sat up, wiped her tears away, and set her chin proudly.

The sun was streaming in when Nick awoke next morning. With surprise he discovered that he was lying downstairs, on a giant cushion, by the remains of the fire. Then it came back to him. Katie. He'd made love to her, and she'd come into his arms, shining, young and beautiful.

Eagerly he turned to her, wanting to embrace her and speak of love. But he found himself alone.

He climbed to his feet and surveyed the scene. A wine bottle and two glasses stood in the hearth, reminding him how it had all started. He wondered if she was angry.

She had every right to be, yet he couldn't banish the memory of her warmth and eagerness.

He climbed the stairs, calling her name, longing for his first glimpse of her. But there was no sign of her, and when he came down again, dressed, he saw the note waiting for him on the kitchen table. It said simply, *'Gone riding.'*

He frowned. Something jarred about the note. It was prosaic, so unlike his own soaring joy. But he hurried out, jumped into the car and headed for the stables.

In no time he was mounted on Blackie and galloping in the direction they usually took. After a while he saw her, thundering along with her hair streaming out behind her. She was full of life and energy, and he smiled in delight as he urged his horse towards her.

She waved to him from a distance and reined in, smiling as he neared.

'Morning,' she carolled cheerfully. 'Isn't it absolutely gorgeous?'

'It's a lovely day,' he agreed.

'I'll say it is. Nothing like a bit of good, healthy exercise.' She breathed in and out exaggeratedly.

A little frown creased his brow. She was smiling, and yet there was something wrong. She was too bright. He wanted to lean over and kiss her, but her very cheerfulness seemed to warn him off.

'You seem very hearty this morning,' he ventured.

'Never felt better. Shall we gallop?'

'Katie, wait. I must—'

'Let's have a good ride first.'

'No,' he said, through the uneasiness that possessed him. 'We have to talk.'

'What about?'

'What about? Last night we—'

'Oh, that! Goodness, what is there to talk about?'

He stared at her, aghast.

'Nick, it was lovely, honestly, but it didn't mean anything. We were both lonely and depressed, and we just sort of—consoled each other. Now it's time to go back to reality.' She smiled at him. 'There's no need to give it another thought.'

She wheeled away and started to race across country. Nick followed as fast as he could, but his horse was sluggish and couldn't keep up. Even so, he could see that she was galloping hell for leather, in a way that worried him. Katie always went as fast as she dared, but this time she rode recklessly, as though she cared nothing for the consequences. Nick expected every moment to see her fall, and at last it happened.

Terrified, he urged his mount on, but by the time he reached her she was already on her feet and brushing herself.

'Katie!' he yelled, jumping down beside her and trying to take hold of her.

To his astonishment, she sidestepped him. 'I'm fine, Nick, honestly. There's no need to make a fuss. As long as my horse isn't hurt—'

'As long as *you're* not hurt,' he said hoarsely. 'Come here.' He reached out.

This time there was no mistaking the way she backed off, or the fierce look she flung him out of glittering eyes.

'What a flap about nothing,' she said, in the harshest voice he'd ever heard her use. 'I'm fine! Look.' She leapt nimbly into the saddle. 'I'd better go back to the stables now, so that they can check the horse.' She patted the beast's neck. 'Poor old boy. It was all my fault.'

She headed back at a slower pace. Nick could easily

have ridden beside her now, but he hung back, devastated at the way his dream had shattered so quickly. There was no mistaking the message Katie had sent him. The lovemaking that had been a glorious revelation for him had been quite the opposite for her. He knew now that no other man had been before him. He'd beguiled her into giving him something that rightly belonged to her true love. Now she couldn't bear Nick to touch her. She hated him, and she had every right.

When the vet had checked the horse and pronounced him well, they drove back to the cottage in near silence. Katie was looking very pale, but he didn't know how to mention it. He was all at sea.

Suddenly she said, 'I suppose we'd better be getting back to London. How about leaving this afternoon?'

'All right,' he said. He was sick at heart.

On the journey home she chose to sit in the back, claiming to be tired. In his rearview mirror he could see her lying against the seat with her eyes closed. He couldn't tell if she was really asleep, but he doubted it. She looked as if she'd been crying.

He made one last effort when they reached home. At the door of her apartment he said, 'Please, Katie—I'm sorry.'

'There's nothing to be sorry for.'

'You know there is. I'm desperately sorry for last night—it shouldn't have happened—I didn't mean it to, and if you knew how bitterly I regret it—'

She looked at him out of bleak eyes. 'But I do know, Nick. Let's leave it there, shall we? Goodnight.'

She went inside before he could speak. He returned despondently to his own home, wondering how he could have made such a mess of things.

*   *   *

The following week he took over his new job, and plunged into a hectic schedule that left him no time for anything but work. He liked the job. He knew he could do it. But his enjoyment was ruined by the memory of Katie's distraught face, and his own aching heart.

He called Lilian, knowing that there were things to be said between them. But he was saved the trouble. Lilian was a shrewd lady. When he found himself talking to her answer-machine for the third time, and when she didn't reply to any of his calls, he began to get the message. A few nights later he saw her dancing in the arms of a wealthy industrialist who'd just made a huge killing on the stock exchange. She smiled at him distantly, but made no attempt to speak. And so they passed out of each other's lives.

He followed Katie's progress with difficulty. Derek was taking her out again, and had given her a job in his company. As far as Nick could tell, Katie had embarked on a career of dissipation, staying out until all hours and going to every party in sight. Once they found themselves at the same function, and he was shocked by her pallor, the feverishness with which she danced and the wildness of her laughter.

When he tried to talk to her she responded with brittle cheerfulness, asking him about his job but refusing to discuss herself. She seemed determined to keep him at an emotional distance, and he didn't know how to get past her guard. But he had wrought this bitter change in her, and he couldn't forgive himself.

One night, driven beyond endurance, he watched for her arrival and waylaid her on the stairs. She was thinner, and there were dark smudges under her eyes that tore at his heart.

'Katie, it can't go on like this,' he pleaded. 'We have to talk.'

'I don't see why.'

'Because things can't just be left as they have been. I'm sorry for what happened at the cottage—'

'Did something happen?' Katie asked brightly. 'Oh, yes, it's coming back to me, vaguely.'

'Stop that,' he shouted. 'If you hate me for making love to you, at least come out and say so. I'm sorry. I'll do anything to make it right, only please, Katie, don't hate me.'

'Hate you?' Katie echoed in disbelief. 'Hate you?'

He loved her so much, he wanted to gather her into his arms and beg her to love him. Then something in the sight of her face struck him over the heart, and in the same moment came enlightenment.

'That's it!' he said excitedly. 'Now I know. It's always been there, but I didn't understand it before.'

'Whatever are you talking about?'

'Now I know why you've always reminded me of Isobel.'

'Oh, get lost!' she said furiously. 'It's always Isobel with you. You've lived with a ghost all these years, Nick, and, what's worse, it's the ghost of someone who never really existed. But you can't see that, because you don't want to see it.'

'Darling, let me explain—'

'Don't call me darling,' she cried passionately. 'I'm not your darling, and I never can be. Nothing you say means anything.'

'I didn't mean to hurt you,' he said humbly. 'Try to forgive me, even though I'll never forgive myself.'

'You don't know when you're hurting people, Nick. You just don't notice. Go away and leave me alone. I never want to talk to you again. There's nothing left to—nothing I can—' She stopped, choking.

'Katie—' He reached for her, but she flung him off.

'No,' she cried, and fled.

He didn't pursue her. It would have been useless, and besides, his guilt held him there. He thought he'd never seen so much misery in anyone's face as he'd just seen in Katie's. And he, who loved her, had done this to her.

After all this time he'd found his love, the one true love of his life. And now he faced the bitter irony of knowing that he'd lost her in the same moment.

CHAPTER TWELVE

NICK slept badly, and finally awoke out of a fretful doze. He struggled out of bed, feeling as though he'd been dredged up from the sea bed. Derek was already in the kitchen, making toast.

'Want some?' he asked cheerfully.

'Uhuh!'

'I'll take that as a yes. There's some mail for you.'

Nick studied the envelopes. Most of them clearly contained bills. But one was pale blue, bearing Isobel's distinctive hand. The sight didn't give him the usual jolt of pleasure/pain, and he wondered how long it was since that had happened.

It took a moment for his eyes to focus, and then he realised he was reading a sentence halfway down the first page. He read it three times, trying to believe that it really said what he thought it said.

It broke my heart to see you so much in love with Nick, all those years ago.

He rubbed his eyes and went back to the start of the letter. It began, *'Dear Katie…'*

Frowning, he checked the envelope. It bore his name and address. Isobel must have been writing to them both, and put the letters in the wrong envelopes. At this point, he knew, he should virtuously fold Katie's letter away and read no more. He also knew that he had no intention of doing so. Besides, he doubted if Katie was behaving virtuously with *his* letter...

Dear Katie,
It seems ages since you last wrote to me, and I hope that's because everything's going wonderfully, and you're too busy enchanting Nick with your wiles to have time to write.

I think you're so clever to have managed this far without him suspecting anything. But then, dear Nick was always a bit unsuspicious, if you know what I mean. Brilliant with facts and figures, but emotionally he wore blinkers. Otherwise he'd have seen that you had a whopping great crush on him when you were sixteen. Although, since you spent your life trying to wind him up, I suppose he shouldn't be blamed too much.

It broke my heart to see you so much in love with Nick, all those years ago. But when you came back from Australia the ugly duckling had turned into a swan, and I was sure he must fall in love with you.

I admit I had my doubts when you suggested going to London, and me asking Nick to look after you. It was a clever way of getting his attention, but I'd hoped you might have grown out of him. Or that when you saw him again you'd realise you'd been loving a dream. But you say you're as crazy about him as ever.

You've handled it brilliantly so far. Getting him to take you to the cottage was good (dear Patsy's always been so kind and helpful), although it was a little naughty of you to let Nick get the wrong idea about Jake.

By the way, Jake came here a couple of days ago. He seems a very nice young man. He told me about

*his theory that you'd been in love with someone all
along, so I told him who it was, and he said he
guessed he 'hadn't been very bright about that'. I said
not to worry, because Nick hasn't been very bright
about it either.*

*Call me soon and let me know how you're doing.
I look forward to being matron of honour at your
wedding. I just hope Nick doesn't hurt you again...*

Slowly Nick put the letter down, feeling as if all the
breath had been knocked out of him. It was a conspiracy,
with himself as the victim. Everything Katie had said or
done since coming here had been towards one end; putting a ring through his nose and leading him up the aisle
like a lamb to the slaughter, with Isobel and Patsy sing-
ing hosannas all the way.

How quickly his heart had softened to her, how tender
she'd made him feel, how enchanting she'd been! And
he'd fallen for it, hook, line and sinker! The clouds of
disbelief that had been protecting his brain parted
abruptly and his feelings reached the surface in a bellow
of outrage.

'Hey!' Derek choked over his toast and began frantically mopping his tea. 'What's up with you?'

'It's a conspiracy,' Nick seethed. 'Katie set me up.'

'Good grief, have you only just discovered that?'

Nick turned wild eyes upon him. 'You *knew*?'

'I knew Katie was crazy about you half an hour after
I met her. I should think Patsy knew in ten minutes.'

'My friends,' Nick said bitterly.

'I took Katie to dinner and she told me everything:
how she fell for you when she was sixteen but you only
had eyes for Isobel.'

'So that was it! I always knew she was conniving to
separate Isobel and me—'

'Forget it. If Isobel had loved you Katie couldn't have done a thing about it.'

'Well, she really managed to get you on her side!'

'Sure she did. I promised to help out. She was obviously what you needed to stop you becoming a mean, miserable old man.'

Nick eyes glinted. 'You're saying that all that stuff between you was just an act? When you kept her out until all hours, and then smooched like there was no tomorrow—it was all for my benefit?'

'Katie wouldn't kiss me for any other reason,' Derek admitted sadly. 'It's you she loves. Don't ask me why.' He grinned. 'It worked too. You hated seeing her in my arms.'

'I hated seeing her fall into the hands of a bad character like you.'

'Stop kidding yourself. You were jealous as hell. Not that it achieved anything. When I think of the work your friends put in to save you from yourself—all wasted because you're too blind to see when a gorgeous, sexy girl is mad about you, and too dumb to love her back—'

'What are you talking about?' Nick snapped. 'Of course I love her.'

'Then what's got your goat? Katie's madly in love with you. What more do you want?'

'That's not the…' Nick's voice faded, and he stared into space. The world shifted on its axis. Suddenly all his confusion was gone and everything was beautifully simple. Ahead of him was a sunlit landscape, and at his feet was the path that led to Katie, and her love.

And what a love: steady and true through the years, without hope, from the other side of the world. Katie loved him. *Katie loved him!*

He was out of the door in an instant, running up the

stairs to her apartment, holding his finger on the bell. At last the door was opened by Leonora.

'I need to see Katie, quickly,' Nick said.

'Sorry, she's gone.'

'When will she be back?'

'She won't. She's gone.'

A cold hand clutched at the pit of his stomach. 'Gone?' he echoed stupidly.

'Yes. Gone, as in "gone". Last night. Clutching a suitcase. For ever. She looked pretty unhappy to me. Are you the jerk who did that to her?'

'Yes,' he said, dazed. 'I'm the jerk who did that to her. Please, did she say where she was going?'

'Only that she was leaving "for foreign parts".'

He managed a shaky smile. 'She never could resist a touch of the dramatic,' he said fondly. 'But she must have said something more specific.'

'Well, she didn't,' Leonora said, eyeing him with disfavour. 'Just "foreign parts". And there's an awful lot of them.'

She shut the door, leaving him aghast.

He found Derek just leaving the flat. 'You're back quickly.'

'She wasn't there,' Nick said frantically. 'She's vanished abroad without leaving an address. She went last night.'

'Don't panic. "Abroad" probably means Australia. No good dashing to the airport now. She'll have taken off. But you can check the flights for when she's landing and take it from there. Look, I have to go. I'll be away a few days. Perhaps I should stay. You look like a man in a crisis.'

Nick pulled himself together. 'No, I'm fine. You're right about Australia. I'll find her.' He remembered that

Katie and Derek were in cahoots. 'If she should contact you, tell her that I—just say that—hell!'

Derek regarded him with pity. 'I'll tell her,' he said.

As soon as he reached the office Nick started calling airlines with flights to Australia, but passenger lists were confidential, and no amount of arguing could get him the information he wanted. Finally he slammed the receiver down, and sat with his head slumped. When he looked up, Patsy was setting a cup of strong coffee before him.

'I suppose you know all about it?' he growled.

'I know you've made poor Katie very unhappy, but she wouldn't tell me any details.'

'You've spoken to her?'

'She called me last night, but she didn't mention Australia. In fact she didn't say she was going away.'

'What did she say?' Nick asked eagerly.

'Only that she'd finally accepted that you'd never love her because you still love Isobel.'

'Nonsense!'

'That's what I told her, but I don't think she took it in. She sounded as if she'd been crying.'

'Patsy, what am I going to do? She's gone abroad somewhere, but they won't check the flight lists for me.'

'Of course not. For that you need subtlety. Call Amos Renbury on this number.' She wrote it down. 'He's a private investigator who specialises in anything to do with transport. Mention my name. He owes me a favour.'

Patsy's name worked wonders. Amos was immediately anxious to be obliging, but when he called back half an hour later it was to report a blank. Katie's name wasn't on a flight list to Australia or anywhere else. Nor had she booked for a ferry or the Channel Tunnel. Amos flatly refused to accept a fee, leaving Nick wondering just how Patsy had put him in her debt.

'Patsy,' he said in awe, 'I'm beginning to realise I've never known anything about you.'

While they'd waited for Amos's call he'd told her about the letter. Now she regarded him with fond exasperation. 'Nick, dear, you've never known anything about anybody. That's why you're in this mess. Try Isobel.'

But Isobel too had no idea where Katie was, and she was outraged with Nick.

'You can't seriously blame me for not falling for Katie when she was sixteen,' he protested.

'Of course not. She was just a kid, and she hadn't grown up to her best.'

'I'll say!'

'Well, it wasn't her fault she looked like a broom handle at my wedding,' Isobel said defensively. 'Blue satin is something she should never wear.'

'It wasn't her looks. It was the way she constantly attacked me with every weapon she could find, words, elbows…'

'She did that to get your attention. Once she said, "At least when he's mad at me, he knows I'm there." And all the time she was in Australia she made me write about you, and send photos. I thought her feelings would die a natural death, especially when Dad said she'd grown so lovely that she could have any young man she wanted. But all she wanted was you. Then she came back, so beautiful, and still so set on you, even after all this time.'

'But you deceived me,' Nick said, belatedly remembering that he was aggrieved. 'Those things you said when you wrote and asked me to look after her—'

'That was Katie's letter. It took her hours to get it right. I just copied it out.'

Nick stood speechless, appalled by the perfidy of women.

'I thought everything was going so well between you,' Isobel said reproachfully. 'Whatever did you do to drive her away?'

'How come I'm to blame?'

'You were supposed to be looking after her. Now she's wandering about, lonely and miserable, with nowhere to go. I think that makes you very much to blame. How could you be so blind as not to see she was in love with you?'

'Because I've always thought of myself as in love with you,' he said, goaded.

'Oh, Nick, don't be absurd! You were never really in love with me. You just liked adoring me from afar, with no danger of having to commit yourself. When you're faced with a flesh and blood woman who really wants you, you back off. If anything happens to poor little Katie I shall hold you entirely responsible.'

Nick was left staring at a dead phone.

'Why has everyone decided it's my fault?' he demanded.

'That's easy,' Patsy said. 'It *is* your fault. We all tried to help you see the light.'

'Oh, yes, you were in the conspiracy too, weren't you?'

'I did my bit. I moved out of your flat when Derek left so that you and Katie could be alone together. I fixed you up with the cottage. I kept Lilian away.

'Katie made you happy, Nick, and that improved you so much. You lightened up, started laughing, even made jokes. It was obvious she was the right girl. All your

friends rallied around and did their best for you—and
you blew it!'

The flat was appallingly quiet that night. It had been
quiet the last time Katie had left, but that was different.
Then he hadn't known what he'd lost. Now he understood the full disaster. He loved Katie. More than that,
he idolised her, worshipped her. She'd brought him to
life, filling his world with joy. And how had he repaid
her for these glorious gifts? By breaking her heart and
driving her away. Now she was wandering somewhere,
perhaps without even a roof over her head.

Isobel's accusation—'You just liked adoring me from
afar, with no danger of having to commit yourself'—
still stung him. Was that really a true picture of himself?

He remembered something Derek had said when he'd
first learned about Isobel, 'So that's your excuse for
avoiding commitment. A damned convenient excuse, if
you ask me!'

Had his fidelity to Isobel been no more than a way of
staying detached? Or had he subconsciously been waiting for Katie to grow up? He would have been glad to
believe that. It might make him feel less of a heel than
he did at this moment. But he wasn't sure anything
would make him feel that.

He lay awake for hours, and when he finally began to
nod off a noise startled him awake again. He sat up,
straining his ears. He could hear nothing, but something
in the quality of the silence told him he wasn't alone.

Then came a faint, muffled sound from the next room.
He was out of bed fast, pulling the door open a crack
and listening. Now he could hear the soft sound of
breathing. Perhaps Derek had returned? No, he would
have put the light on.

Moving noiselessly, he pulled the door wide. The moonlight from the windows gave him a good view of the apartment, but the intruder was in shadow against the far wall. Nick could hear breathing, and footsteps that were nearing the door of what had been Katie's room.

The thought of a burglar ransacking the place where Katie had slept made the blood rush to his head. He launched himself forward and collided with another body. It was smaller than he'd expected, but it fought vigorously and nearly winded him. He gasped, struggling to get both arms about the flailing creature, but just as he succeeded Katie's door opened and they fell through, reeling across the room to collapse together on the bed.

'*Now!*' Nick said, fumbling for the switch to the bed-side lamp. 'You'd better have a damned good explan—' His voice died.

The intruder's pale face looked up at him from the pillow. 'Hallo, Nick.'

'Katie? What in thunder are you doing—? *Katie!*' Forgetting all else but his heartfelt relief, he scooped her up into his arms and held her close. 'Oh, Katie, Katie!'

She clung to him wordlessly, and turned her face up to his. He kissed her urgently, again and again, trying to reassure himself that she was really there.

'I've been out of my mind with worry,' he said hoarsely. 'What do you mean by frightening me like that? I thought it was a burglar. I might have hurt you.'

'More likely I'd have hurt you. I was winning that little fight.'

'In your dreams!'

They glared at each other, but Nick didn't release her, nor did she try to free herself from his arms.

'Katie, where have you been? I've been searching all over for you. I thought you'd gone for good.'

'I *have* gone for good.'

'Oh, no, you haven't,' he said, keeping hold of her.

'I have. I meant to slip in and out without you knowing anything about it. I'm not really here.'

'You feel real enough to me, but perhaps I'd better make sure.' He kissed her again, fiercely, possessively, telling her of his love without words. Katie kissed him back with eager passion.

'You're here, all right,' he said unsteadily. 'And you're going to stay here, with me, for ever.'

'Nick, I can't—'

'Have you been back to the flat upstairs?'

'No.'

'You should. There's a letter for you from Isobel. It starts, *"Dear Nick"*. She wrote to me at the same time, and mine starts, *"Dear Katie"*.'

'You've got my letter?'

'That's a moot point, since the envelope is addressed to me. I wouldn't have missed reading it for the world.'

'What did it say?' Katie asked, a tad nervously.

'You can read it.'

He fetched the letter and gave it to her. Katie scanned the sheets quickly before letting them fall. She couldn't meet Nick's eyes.

'Well?' he asked quietly. 'Is it true?'

Katie nodded. 'It seemed like a good idea at the time. I thought, when we met again, you might like me better. Or at least I could make something happen while I was sharing your flat.'

'All those years ago, when you were acting like I was Public Enemy Number One...'

She gave a watery laugh. 'I did everything I could to

distract you from Isobel. I had to stop you getting married. While I was in Australia I made her tell me all the news about you, and I kept dreading to hear that you'd married someone else. You never did, and I began to hope. But when I came back you were still in love with her.'

'I got over Isobel a long time ago,' he said gently. 'It took me too long to understand that, but now I know who I truly love.'

'Oh, Nick, when did you know it?'

'I began to get the first inkling when we found that little girl, and I saw your wonderful heart. Or maybe it was always there, making me jealous of Derek, of every man you smiled at. I told myself I was taking you to the cottage to protect you from Jake, but actually I just wanted to be alone with you.

'Then Jake told me about this man you loved. I never guessed it was me, and I was miserable and jealous, because I wanted you to love me. And when we made love I dared to hope that you did.'

'But why didn't you tell me?'

'I was going to next morning, but you fended me off. I thought you were angry because you loved another man. If it wasn't that, what was it?'

'You talk in your sleep. I heard you telling Isobel that you were sorry.'

'Only for not loving her any more, because I loved you.'

'I didn't know. I thought you were feeling guilty that you'd betrayed her with me. It had been so wonderful making love with you, and then I heard you saying sorry to her, and I thought—'

A tremor went through her, and he gathered her close again. 'I'll never make you unhappy again,' he vowed fervently. 'I can't get over what I've done to you all this time. When we drove back from the cottage I thought you hated me.'

'I couldn't hate you, Nick. I love you. I always have and I always will. Since we came back I've felt I ought to go away and try to get you out of my system. But I never could. I kept hanging on for one last moment with you. And when we did speak it all went wrong, and I found myself attacking you.'

'Just like old times,' he said with a smile. 'Will we ever stop fighting, Katie? Or when we're old and grey, with a dozen grandchildren, will you still be winding me up for the fun of it?'

'Of course, because you'll still be asking for it. There was a moment last night when I wondered if you were beginning to understand, but then you went off at a tangent about Isobel and me having something in common.'

'But you have. I'd just realised what it was—I fell in love with both of you in the first moment. I had that feeling when we met at the station, and it's haunted me ever since. And suddenly I knew what it meant. I tried to tell you, but you stormed off.'

'I thought it was no good, and you'd never love me. I was going to go abroad and never see you again.'

'I checked, but you weren't on any of the passenger lists.'

Katie gave a watery chuckle. 'I was going to leave it to chance. I went to the airport, meaning to get the first plane going anywhere.'

'What changed your mind?'

'I found I didn't have my passport. And then I remembered. When I left here to go to that hostel I packed in a hurry, and I didn't empty the top drawer of my bedside table. My passport was in there. That's why I had to come back.'

'You forgot your passport?' Nick said slowly, unable to believe his ears.

'Well, you know me. Always losing things, or forgetting them, or muddling everything up. You can't marry me, Nick. I'm a burden to you; you know I am. I'll turn your life into chaos.'

'It'll be beautiful chaos,' he said, regarding her tenderly. His lips twitched. 'You set out to explore the world, and you forgot your passport.'

'It could happen to anybody,' she said with dignity.

Suddenly the laugh that had been welling up in him exploded to the surface. He gathered her into his arms and they rocked back and forth together.

'No, it couldn't,' he choked. 'It could only happen to you, to my beautiful, unpredictable Katie, my maddening, adorable Katie. Kiss me, Katie! Kiss me and love me for ever and a day. *Oh, my darling Katie!*'

Take 2 bestselling love stories FREE

Plus get a FREE surprise gift!

Special Limited-Time Offer

Mail to Harlequin Reader Service®

3010 Walden Avenue
P.O. Box 1867
Buffalo, N.Y. 14240-1867

YES! Please send me 2 free Harlequin Romance® novels and my free surprise gift. Then send me 6 brand-new novels every month, which I will receive months before they appear in bookstores. Bill me at the low price of $2.90 each plus 25¢ delivery and applicable sales tax if any*. That's the complete price, and a saving of over 10% off the cover prices—quite a bargain! I understand that accepting the books and gift places me under no obligation ever to buy any books. I can always return a shipment and cancel at any time. Even if I never buy another book from Harlequin, the 2 free books and the surprise gift are mine to keep forever.

116 HEN CH66

Name	(PLEASE PRINT)	
Address	Apt. No.	
City	State	Zip

This offer is limited to one order per household and not valid to present Harlequin Romance® subscribers. *Terms and prices are subject to change without notice. Sales tax applicable in N.Y.

UROM-98

©1990 Harlequin Enterprises Limited

Question: How do you find the
red-hot cowboy of your dreams?

Answer: Read on....

Texas Men Wanted! is a brand-new
miniseries in Harlequin Romance®.

Meet three very special heroines who are all looking for
very special Texas men—their future husbands! They've all
signed up with the Yellow Rose Matchmakers. The Yellow
Rose guarantees to find any woman her perfect partner....

So for the cutest cowboys in the whole state of Texas,
look out for:

HAND-PICKED HUSBAND
by Heather MacAllister in January 1999

BACHELOR AVAILABLE!
by Ruth Jean Dale in February 1999

THE NINE-DOLLAR DADDY
by Day Leclaire in March 1999

Available wherever
Harlequin Romance books are sold.

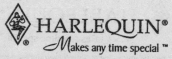

HARLEQUIN®

Makes any time special ™

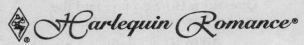

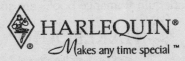

For a limited time, Harlequin and Silhouette have an offer you just can't refuse.

In November and December 1998:

BUY **ANY** TWO HARLEQUIN
OR SILHOUETTE BOOKS and
SAVE $10.00
off future purchases

OR BUY ANY THREE HARLEQUIN OR SILHOUETTE BOOKS
AND **SAVE $20.00** OFF FUTURE PURCHASES!

(each coupon is good for $1.00 off the purchase of two
Harlequin or Silhouette books)

....

JUST BUY 2 HARLEQUIN OR SILHOUETTE BOOKS, SEND US YOUR
NAME, ADDRESS AND 2 PROOFS OF PURCHASE (CASH REGISTER
RECEIPTS) AND HARLEQUIN WILL SEND YOU A COUPON BOOKLET
WORTH **$10.00 OFF** FUTURE PURCHASES OF HARLEQUIN OR
SILHOUETTE BOOKS IN 1999. SEND US 3 PROOFS OF PURCHASE AND
WE WILL SEND YOU 2 COUPON BOOKLETS WITH A TOTAL SAVING OF
$20.00. (ALLOW 4-6 WEEKS DELIVERY) OFFER EXPIRES
DECEMBER 31, 1998.

....

I accept your offer! Please send me a coupon booklet(s), to:

NAME: _____

ADDRESS: _____

CITY: _____ STATE/PROV.: _____ POSTAL/ZIP CODE: _____

Send your name and address, along with your cash register
receipts for proofs of purchase, to:

In the U.S.	In Canada
Harlequin Books	Harlequin Books
P.O. Box 9057	P.O. Box 622
Buffalo, NY	Fort Erie, Ontario
14269	L2A 5X3

PHQ4982

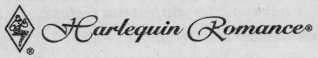

Harlequin Romance®

Coming Next Month

Especially for Christmas we bring you a whole feast of delights.

#3531 READY-MADE BRIDE Janelle Denison

Andrew Fielding wants a mom and his daddy could use a wife. He thinks he's found the perfect woman for both of them: Megan Sanders. Which is fine with Megan—the Fielding men have their attractions: one's as cute as a button, the other's very sexy and, together, they're the family Megan's always wanted! But convincing brooding widower Kane Fielding is less easy....

Whirlwind Weddings—*Who says you can't hurry love?*

#3532 GABRIEL'S MISSION Margaret Way

The way Chloe taunted her boss, Gabriel McGuire, at work could be amusing, but her reckless actions could also be downright exasperating! One of these days she'd take one risk too many. She'd probably worn out a whole host of guardian angels, but some small voice kept telling Gabriel that someone had to protect her and that *he* was the man for the job....

Guardian Angels—*Falling in love sometimes needs a little help from above!*

#3533 ONE NIGHT BEFORE CHRISTMAS Catherine Leigh

When Carly meets Jonah St. John at a Christmas party she decides that all she wants for Christmas this year is the tall, handsome tycoon... gift wrapped! And her wish comes true—at least temporarily. But then Carly learns that Santa's brought her a little something extra this year.... She's having Jonah's baby!

#3534 SANTA'S SPECIAL DELIVERY Val Daniels

Alicia believes that her handsome husband, Daniel, has only married her for their baby's sake, and that he is really in love with another woman. In fact Daniel *is* in love with Alicia, and wants their marriage to last forever—but will he be able to convince her before it's too late...?

Baby Boom—*Because two's company and three (or four or five) is a family!*